EBURY PRESS
INSOMNIA

Rachna Bisht Rawat is the author of five books by Penguin Random House India, including the bestsellers *The Brave* and *Kargil*. She lives in New Delhi with Saransh, the wise teen; Hukum, the bushy-tailed golden retriever; an eclectic collection of books and music; and Manoj, the man in olive green who met her twenty-eight years back, when he was a Gentleman Cadet at the Indian Military Academy, and offered to be her comrade for life. She can be reached at www.rachnabisht.com and rachnabisht@gmail.com. Her Instagram handle is @rachna_bishtrawat.

ADVANCE PRAISE FOR *INSOMNIA*

'A perfect collection of stories about the lives of soldiers in war and peace. Rachna Bisht Rawat has the incredible ability to project how a soldier thinks, talks and acts in diverse situations. A must-read for every citizen of India, especially in these times of tension on our borders'—Major General Ian Cardozo, AVSM, SM

'The settings of Rachna's stories—locales ranging from Siachen, Kashmir, Garhwal to Arunachal—are picture-perfect. Her language, descriptions and similes are masterly. She brings alive her characters and the details of their lives and relationships in the army. Every soldier and his/her spouse will be able to relate closely with each story. This bouquet of stories comprises pathos, tragedy, valour, humour, even wickedness. In one story she writes, "Stories are born in the heart—from seeds quietly sown by people who once walked in and out of it—and can be written only when they start to choke you with their weight." These are stories from the depths of her heart, which could only be written by someone closely related to the army'—General V.P. Malik, PVSM, AVSM, former Chief of Army Staff

'The author's style of writing is easy, lucid and engaging. The bond between two "enemy" soldiers at the army posts on either side of the border, in the story "Saathi", speaks about the vanity of war. The author's affiliation to and affinity for the army comes through with flair in these tales'—Bala Chauhan, *The New Indian Express*

'In these stories laced with humour and pathos, Rachna Bisht Rawat steps away from the heroism of battlefields, as she has been doing in her previous books, to give us a sense of the bittersweet incidents that unfold inside hedge-lined cantonments across the country. A moving portrayal of the lives of soldiers, their families and their brotherhood. Rachna sprinkles her stories with an equal measure of hope and horror, and her lucid prose tells it as it is. This collection should be read by anyone keen to know what lies beneath the olive green' —Deepa Alexander, *The Hindu*

INSOMNIA
ARMY STORIES

Rachna Bisht Rawat

EBURY
PRESS

An imprint of Penguin Random House

EBURY PRESS

USA | Canada | UK | Ireland | Australia
New Zealand | India | South Africa | China

Ebury Press is part of the Penguin Random House group of companies
whose addresses can be found at global.penguinrandomhouse.com

Published by Penguin Random House India Pvt. Ltd
4th Floor, Capital Tower 1, MG Road,
Gurugram 122 002, Haryana, India

Penguin
Random House
India

First published in Ebury Press by Penguin Random House India 2020

ISBN 9780143445838

Typeset in Adobe Garamond Pro by Manipal Technologies Limited, Manipal
Printed at Thomson Press India Ltd, New Delhi

www.penguin.co.in

MIX
Paper
FSC FSC® C010615

For my beautiful mom, Sushila Bisht,
who wanted me to write stories

Contents

Preface

Insomnia is a compilation of stories, many of which I wrote nearly ten years back, in sleepy Ferozepur, the last town of Punjab on the India–Pakistan border. I would drag a chair into the bamboo thicket at the end of our garden and sit there with my laptop, the breeze carrying to me strains of the Gurbani from across the yellow mustard fields.

Though the stories were not getting published anywhere, they added so much meaning to my life. A portion of the book I wrote more recently, in the lonely months of the lockdown, cut away from the world by the pandemic that suddenly changed everything. I would work on it leaning back on the sofa in my Delhi flat, with a steaming mug of tea by my side and a bored Hukum— our handsome golden retriever—dozing off at my feet, his long silken ears brushing the floor. These stories helped take away some of the stifling sadness that had seeped into my heart as I constantly lived and breathed episodes of tragic human loss while writing *Kargil*, my previous book.

This mixed bag of tales will show you a world of olive green that is inhabited not just by heroes but also by characters cut out from the same fabric of society that defines most of us: some strong, some weak, some seeped in moral courage, others twisted and evil. Isn't that how it is in the real world?

The stories I particularly enjoyed writing are the ones about the escapades of a happy-go-lucky major in the Indian Army who is loosely based on a young paratrooper I know. You will find him and his company of badass soldiers navigating their Kashmir and Siachen postings with a devil-may-care attitude. Their (mis)adventures give you a glimpse of how life actually is in the army, where young boys, straight out of college, are ready to risk everything in the line of duty, with a song on their lips and a wicked prank in their heads.

While many of the incidents you will read in this book are based on true events and many of the characters are drawn from people I know, much of what you will read comes with what we, in the writing world, called creative licence. Which means that it is all a product of the writer's imagination and may or may not be true.

Many of these stories were written at a time when I had no contacts in publishing. So I wrote these promising myself that one day, maybe a hundred years later, I would compile them into a book. It seemed like an impossible dream back then, but I guess a hundred years sometimes pass by in the blink of an eye. And dreams do come true. That's what I would like you to take back from this book. So, happy dreaming! And, I hope, some happy reading too!

Courage

Dusk had fallen. The crickets were calling. A translucent moon hung between the trees, climbing slowly into the sky like a scared kid reluctantly stepping into a dark room, not sure of where the light switch was. The evening was still and soaked with post-monsoon moisture. Bisht rubbed a habitual hand along the side of his neck only to find it clammy with sweat. 'Dammit!' He grimaced, wiping his hand along the side of his pants. There had been no time to change. No inclination, actually. He hadn't gone home at all. For a moment, he couldn't even remember if he had had any lunch. He had gone to the mess, he recollected. He had sat alone at the long dining table meant for eighteen people where a plate had been laid out for him; spoon on the right, fork on the left, dessert spoon up front. The hovering mess waiter had quickly served the meal. White porcelain bowls with the blue Para Regiment logo placed size-wise in perfect military precision. Rice. Dal. Sabzi. Chicken curry. Salad. He didn't need to look up. He knew the Wednesday menu by heart.

The mess waiter was walking in with a hot chapati when Bisht had suddenly got up, pushing his chair back, its legs scraping the wood-panelled floor. 'Manohar, mujhe khana nahi khana. Plate hata de,' he had said and, picking up his beret and car keys from the side table, walked out. So that explained the faint rumble in his stomach.

* * *

Lieutenant Colonel Rajnish Bisht, Sena Medal—short, stocky with a smashed boxer's nose and a don't-mess-with-me attitude that automatically made youngsters treat him with respect—squared his shoulders and entered the old building. It used to be a school in British times but was now serving the Indian Army's need for a base hospital. Its grey stone facade had acquired an orange sheen in the setting sun. The first time he had seen the building—its red roof, the sweeping arches and the stark white bougainvillea climbing over the faded stones—it had taken his breath away. Today, he didn't even notice it. Stepping briskly up the steps, he walked down the long, deserted corridor with its dangling light bulbs encased in green tin shades that looked like Chinese fisherman hats and were spilling pools of yellow on his uniform, making the brass lion and stars on his shoulders shine.

His feet found their way to the intensive care unit, taking a complicated series of turns by muscle memory alone. For more than a fortnight, he had been coming here twice every day; thrice if he could find some more time between office hours. He stopped at the sign outside the ICU that said 'No visitors beyond this point', craning his neck to look through the rectangular glass panel in the door. His brain knew what sight awaited him. It was as if a movie had been paused at a moment in time, fifteen days back. On a sanitized white bed lay his company second-in-command, Major Abhay Singh Rathore, Shaurya Chakra, Scna Medal, still and almost lifeless. He was on a ventilator. Bisht watched him quietly, just as he had been doing every day. The lump in his throat felt heavier.

* * *

The doctor had been frank with him. Rathore's condition had worsened considerably. The chances of him making it through the next twelve hours were very slim. 'Be with his parents. They will need you,' the doctor had told Bisht.

It was going to be a long night. Bisht continued to look in through the glass, taking in every detail of Rathore's angular face, drained of all colour, the cheekbones more prominent than ever before, the lips pale and bloodless. His eyes were shut, his head was swathed in white bandage and transparent tubes had been inserted into his nose and mouth. The rest of his tall, lanky frame was covered with white sheets looping and falling over the contours of his body. The bugger had never been this still in his life. 'If you could see yourself now, you'd be ashamed. Get up, bastard. We need you alive,' Bisht thought aloud, his eyes clouding with tears.

On either side of the bed sat Rathore's parents—thin, grey-haired retired Brigadier G.S. Rathore, Sena Medal, Vishisht Seva Medal, on one side and a tired-looking, dishevelled Mrs Vimla Rathore on the other. Each had grasped one of Abhay's hands tightly, as if trying to help him hold on to the life that the surgeon said could ebb out of him anytime. For a moment, Bisht considered going in but then decided against it, granting the old couple the privacy to grieve alone in what could be the last hours of their only son's life.

* * *

Running a hand over his tired eyes, he sat down to wait on the wooden bench outside the ICU, crossed arms resting loosely on his chest. He could sense a migraine attack coming and leant his head back, feeling the hard wood pressing into the nape of his neck, where his crew cut ended and the shirt collar started. He had hardly slept in the past few days. Each time he shut his eyes, a dozen different images of Rathore assaulted his senses, driving sleep away. Initially he had tried to distract himself but since that didn't seem to help, he had given up. Now he would just watch his thoughts come and go, observing them like a man in meditation. The only difference was that each time they came, they seemed to cut his soul with a knife, adding to the searing, almost physical pain he was suffering from.

This time he saw Rathore in Kashmir—an untidy stubble on his chin, face streaked with grime, gaunt from days spent climbing craggy mountains on tinned rations, scraping gunpowder off fallen snow and sucking on it when the mouth got dry. Unkempt but still looking gorgeous. 'Abey model bann na tha tujhe, saale, fauj mein kyun aa gaya marne,' Bisht thought aloud, a sad smile on his lips. Rathore was standing against a rock face, grinning wickedly, his dark eyes shining. 'Jalte ho, sir, meri good looks se. Mujhe maaloom hai.'

And then, the memory that flashed before his eyes every single day. Rathore bending over to tie a shoelace and saying, 'I'm not afraid of enemy bullets, sir.' Then standing up with a divine smile, distributing gyan. 'There can only be one bullet with my name written on it. Why fear the others. Buzdil sau bar marte hain, bahadur bas ek baar.' Bisht rolling his eyes. 'Aisa Papa kehte hain, sir. He fought in the 1965 war, then again in '71. Came back home safe each time. Ek goli toh zarur hogi jis pe mera naam likha hoga, par baaki se main nahi darta.'

Bisht felt the bile rise in his throat and stifled an urge to vomit. The migraine had hit him quick and hard, catching his unawares, like a good boxer. He raised his hands to his forehead and pressed so hard with his fingers that he felt they might just slice into his brain.

* * *

At his lonely vigils outside the ICU over the past days, Bisht's mind presented before his eyes almost every single memory he had of Rathore. Some had surprised him, because they had been lying buried so deep in the cobwebs of time that he had forgotten they existed.

Rathore joining the unit as a lieutenant eight years back—slim, good-looking and with that familiar swagger of immortality that all young officers who have not seen action come with. Rathore during the unit's Northeast deployment—interrogating militants, leading cordon-and-search operations, fierce, unafraid, taking risks that an experienced soldier never would. Rathore during the Kargil war, insolent and reckless, enjoying the thrill of putting his life at risk for his country. Sitting in a crevice, his rifle beside him, eating five-day-old dry puris, joking that they were better than his mom's cooking. Volunteering for the most difficult operations, returning from one and then insisting that he accompany Bisht on another, to flush out intruders from Peak 5412—his eyes red from lack of sleep, face sunburnt, skin peeling off from being constantly whipped by the icy wind.

'Bloody Rathore, you are tired. You are not coming with us. Stay back.'

'Nahi thakaa, sir. I am not letting you do this alone.'

That legendary daylight attack when they had managed to storm and take over an enemy-occupied post after killing four enemy soldiers and capturing one. They had brought back a stash of weapons and rations, with zero casualties on their own side, earning the regiment a battle honour and getting both of them a Sena Medal each.

And finally, Rathore back from the war, celebrating his own invincibility—in the bar at Dum Pukht, the classiest five-star restaurant in the city, coaxing a voluptuous Russian girl to dance with him, cheerfully egged on by the other bachelors.

Rathore had built up a formidable reputation over these few years. He had always led from the front, had stood by his men, and he had proven himself both in peace and in war. During Kargil, he had carried on his back a soldier, who had his leg blown off by a landmine, down to safety. In Agra, he had withdrawn money from his Defence Services Officers Provident Fund and handed it over, with a magnanimous 'Jab honge, lauta dena', to his man Friday, whose sister was getting married.

As captain of the football team, he had brought the Inter Regimental Football Cup home every tournament, including once when he had fractured his arm during practice but had stood in the audience with his arm in plaster and screamed his head off, cheering his team to victory.

He featured frequently in the langar gup. When he cracked jokes with soldiers much older than him and addressed them with crass expletives, they were flattered by the sense of familiarity he evoked in them. At the Regimental Bara Khana, they would hold out their plates for him, coaxing him to pick up the best morsels of meat. They would load his glass with one large rum after another and ensure that he returned to his room drunk and whistling. The men doted on him and did mental calculations about whether they would be lucky enough to serve with him when he took over the command of the unit.

When he left the unit on posting, promising to be back in two years, the Charlie Company's Junior Commissioned Officer had given a heartwarming speech, saying how every man in the company had 'ek aankh mein sukh ka aansu, ek aankh mein dukh ka aansu, kyunki sa'ab promotion pe jaa raha hai, par hame chor ke jaa raha hai'. He also emphasized how Rathore had been an example to everyone, 'Sa'ab ek namune ki tarah raha.' A laughing Rathore had accepted it all and had promised them that he would be back soon.

* * *

In his eight years with the regiment, Rathore had done two terms in Kashmir and had two gallantry awards to show for those. When the regiment was being de-inducted from Kashmir for a well-deserved peacetime posting, word got around that the Brigade Commander was looking for an officer to act as a guide for the new unit coming to replace them. This man should know the area like the back of his hand and stay back to guide the new battalion for a month. No one was surprised when Rathore's name came up. He had no complaints. 'The girls will be heartbroken, sir. Do tell them I shall be there soon,' he had quipped, bidding farewell to Bisht, who got into his Jonga to lead the convoy of happy soldiers to Srinagar, from where they would catch a flight back home.

After a few days of moving around villages that were dens of militant activity and introducing the new unit to informers and vice versa, Rathore's task was effectively over. He was just waiting for the time to pass and his date of leave to arrive when one morning, information came that a suspected militant was visiting a nearby village. A cordon-and-search operation was ordered. Since Rathore knew the area best, he offered to lead with two soldiers.

Walking in single file, the three closed in on the suspected hut. Suddenly, a shot rang out and a bullet ripped right through Rathore's neck. He clutched his throat, puzzled by the patch of red staining his hand, not realizing that he had been shot. Rifleman Laxman Das, just behind him, fell without a word. The bullet had gone right through Rathore and had lodged in Laxman's heart. The third soldier was quick to react and shot the militant, who was visible at the window for a split second. Rathore turned around and mouthed 'Shabaash!' before sinking to the ground, the blood gushing from his throat staining the soil a dirty red.

While Das died on the spot, the profusely bleeding Rathore was evacuated to Chandigarh. Doctors were amazed to find that the bullet had missed both his trachea and food pipe. Rathore survived and returned to the regiment a hero. He was received at the railway station with great fanfare. The unit band, which had made an exception and specially practised a song that was not in their repertoire, played 'Piya Tu Ab Toh Aaja' on the platform, much to the amusement of other passengers. The soldiers loaded a grinning Rathore with marigold garlands, whose weight made his neck bend. He was lifted out of his railway coach by the young officers of the unit, carried on their shoulders to the Commanding Officer's 'Number 1' Gypsy waiting outside. He had marched into the office of his Company Commander, making him look up from his files with a stomp of his boot and a crisp salute. 'Jai Hind, sir! Major Rathore reporting back to the unit, sir!' Bisht had looked up to find him grinning from ear to ear . . .

There were so many memories of Rathore, and Bisht's brain seemed to have put them on shuffle play. However, the one memory it tended to play on loop was the last one, from just fifteen days back.

* * *

There had been persistent bell-ringing, and he had opened the door to find Rathore standing before him, in faded jeans and a white Egyptian cotton shirt—handsome, smiling, with a whiff of expensive after-shave about him. He was holding a carnation for 'ma'am' and a box of chocolates for the kids. 'You may call it a bribe, sir. But I'm having dinner with you. The mess cook has been trying to poison me with soggy bhindi ki sabzi and lauki.'

'Aaja aaja. Aaj hamare ghar mein bhi kaddu bana hai,' Bisht's wife said to him, laughing.

'No, ma'am, you can't do this to me,' Rathore cried out in mock horror.

They sat on the stringed white garden chairs till late in the night, their shoes acquiring wet patches from the dew on the grass, sharing a bottle of Old Monk, breathing in the musky odour of Rathore's cigarette mixed with the sweetness of the freshly flowered jasmine. Eventually, they decided to leave the unfinished bottle for the weekend and went in for dinner. Rathore left around midnight, complimenting Bisht's wife on the best dinner he had ever had in his life. He ruffled their daughter's hair, saying he had to go get some sleep. 'Goodnight, sir. I have an early morning duty at the firing range.'

* * *

Bisht lifted his sore head from the hard bench. Rolling his eyes to keep sleep out of them, he glanced at his watch. More than an hour had passed. He got up and walked to the ICU one more time. Rathore's mother had fallen asleep, with his limp hand in hers. Ringlets of dry, henna-dyed hair had escaped from her bun, spilling on her tired, tear-stained face. Brigadier Rathore was stroking his son's other hand gently, staring vacantly into space. His face looked haggard and drawn, his eyes dark with suffering. In one week he seemed to have aged ten years. Bisht took off his DMS boots, peeled off his socks, squeezed a fat blob of sanitizer on his palm and after rubbing it on his hands carefully, knocked gently on the door and walked in. Brigadier Rathore looked up at him absent-mindedly.

Bisht mumbled a greeting, at which the old soldier nodded. 'Shall I get you some coffee, sir,' he whispered.

Brigadier Rathore shook his head and then gestured to Bisht that he would be coming out for a smoke. Gently caressing his comatose son's hand one more time, he pulled the sheet over it and followed Bisht out into the corridor. 'Abhay's mother is finally sleeping after two days. I don't want to disturb her,' he said, drawing out a cigarette from his shirt pocket. Lighting up, he led Bisht to the bench. 'If you don't mind, son, can you tell me one more time what happened that day?' he asked, his tired eyes fixed on the glowing end of the cigarette.

* * *

'Rathore—I mean, Abhay—was in charge of firing practice that day, sir,' Bisht said, his voice clear and emotionless. The Brigadier listened intently, his eyes fixed on Bisht's face, a steady hand holding the burning cigarette away. 'Two sections of ten soldiers each were shooting at the same range. After the first detail had fired, Abhay gave them the "khali kar" command and went to check the targets to record performances. Just as he was returning, one of the rifles went off as it had not emptied effectively. This bullet hit the wall, ricocheted and caught Abhay in the back of his head,' Bisht said, his voice steady.

Brigadier Rathore met his gaze unwaveringly. 'Has the man who shot Abhay been identified?'

'Yes, sir. It would have been very difficult to identify which rifle had fired but he came forward on his own.'

'Do you suspect foul play?' the Brigadier asked.

'No, sir. The men loved him. It was a very unfortunate accident but, of course, a court of inquiry has been ordered.'

'Where is the boy who shot Abhay?'

'Probably outside, sir,' Bisht replied. 'He has been coming to the hospital every evening. He is shattered.'

Brigadier Rathore sat still for a while, his arm resting along the back of the bench. 'Call him here,' he said finally. Bisht took quick strides across the long corridor and returned a few minutes later, followed by a slim, slightly built young soldier in army fatigues. Not older than twenty, the boy marched down to the bench where the Brigadier was sitting, stood at attention and saluted him smartly.

'Mujhse bahut badi galti ho gayi sahab,' the boy wept, his voice breaking.

The old man stubbed his cigarette on the arm of the bench and stood up. He looked at the tears streaming down the boy's young face, his swollen red eyes, his shaking shoulders, and bent down slightly, straining to read his nameplate. 'Kedar Singh,' Brigadier Rathore said haltingly. He then drew himself up, his face emotionless. 'Paratrooper Kedar Singh. Teri galti nahin thi, beta. Apne aap ko maaf kar de.' Taking a step forward, he patted the weeping soldier on his back. 'Ja, ghar ja. Khana kha ke so ja, aur kal se duty join kar.'

With that, the Brigadier turned around, dry-eyed, his frail back ramrod straight. 'This is not how Abhay would have liked to die but the bloody bullet had his name written on it,' he said softly and walked back to the ICU with heavy steps. Bisht lowered himself on to the bench, staring blindly ahead.

Saathi

Lance Naik Javed Aziz of the 64 Northern Light Infantry was feeling lonelier than usual that morning. He had been on the glacier for more than two months. Not a single letter from home had reached him on his cold, desolate, inaccessible post, the last on the Pakistan–India border; and he was missing his young wife and newborn daughter so much that even thinking about them brought tears to his eyes. All around him, as far as the eyes could see, there was an ocean of white. Beautiful but barren, Siachen, at 19,000 feet, was often called the highest battlefield in the world. In October, it was lashed by cold winds that could take the skin off people's faces, which was why soldiers kept themselves completely covered when they stepped outside their bunkers.

Javed pulled down his thick monkey cap so that it not just shielded his face right up to the eyebrows but also fit snugly, like a mask, around his neck and mouth, leaving just his nose and eyes uncovered. He peered through the fluorescent-purple Cortina sunglasses that he was wearing.

About 250 metres below him, he could see the fibre-glass hut that marked India's last post on the glacier. Midway between him and that post, Pakistan's boundary ended and India's began. An Indian soldier, also on guard duty just like him, stood outside the hut. He, too, was completely covered in a thick, heavy snowsuit that Javed knew Indians called 'bhaloo suit' because it made one look like a big furry bear. And like Javed, he too wore a woolen balaclava and large UV ray-protection sunglasses.

Almost identically dressed for the cold, unforgiving terrain, the two soldiers faced each other every day. Their task was to keep an eye on the enemy post and report if they noticed any activity or transgression across the mutually agreed boundary between the two countries. On that freezing morning, when the temperature had dipped particularly low—to seventeen degrees below zero—and the icy wind whipped their faces, the two of them seemed to be the only living creatures in the vast white expanse of Siachen. And that was probably what made Lance Naik Javed Aziz reach out to the enemy.

* * *

'Saathi,' he called out loudly, startling himself even more than the soldier who stood 250 metres away, behind a protective wall of ice.

Rifleman Satyapal of 30 Kumaon, just twenty-two years old and on his second posting, raised his head to look at where the voice had come from. He was surprised to find the Pakistani soldier waving at him. They were forbidden to interact with the enemy in any way, so Satyapal pointedly ignored him and started looking in the other direction.

'Hamse kuch guftagu toh kar lo, miyan. Madhuri Dixit nahi maang rahe aapse.' The Pakistani soldier had a mischievous ring to his voice.

Satyapal found himself smiling in spite of his reservations. He had been standing in the freezing cold for two hours. There was still another hour to go before guard duty changed and another man replaced him outside the ten-by-eight-feet bunker, within which his five comrades and Post Commander were ensconced, relatively comfortable in the warmth generated by the kerosene stove burning 24/7 inside.

Shifting his rifle to a more comfortable place on his shoulder, he looked at the Pakistani soldier higher up on the slope. 'Madhuri Dixit ke bare mein sochna bhi mat. Tumhare liye ham Dharmendra baithe hain yahan,' he called out, alert and ready to duck if the enemy soldier lifted his rifle to fire at him.

'Rakh lo, miyan, rakh lo. Hamare paas hamari begum hain.'

A deep chuckle reached Satyapal's ear, effortlessly crossing the boundary between the two warring nations. It held no threats, just the promise of easy camaraderie. He liked the sound of it and waved back. And that was how Lance Naik Javed Aziz of the Northern Light Infantry and Rifleman Satyapal of 30 Kumaon, expected to be arch-enemies, became friends on the highest battlefield in the world.

* * *

They soon realized that they were both on the 9 a.m. to 12 noon guard-duty shifts. Inside their respective, well-insulated bunkers, their comrades could not hear what was going on outside, and really didn't worry about it either. Both sides knew that on Siachen, the weather was your real enemy and not another country. So no one cared if rules about zero interaction with the enemy were being broken.

The two of them had complete freedom for conversations, which took away some of their stifling loneliness. 'Kaise ho, saathi?' Satyapal would call out soon after he stepped out of his bunker to invariably find Javed already keeping watch from his.

'Walekum assalaam, saathi,' Javed would respond warmly. 'Khairiyat hai.' The two of them would then spend their time in innocuous conversation about films they had seen, people they loved, dreams they nurtured.

Occasionally, the two enemy posts would fire at each other. The two saathis would be party to it. They would shoot rocket launchers at each other's posts and exchange artillery and mortar fire, sending the snow flying and making the snow-clad mountains reverberate with the sound of gunfire. But the next morning both would be back to their duties, ready for another round of amicable conversation.

* * *

'Eid mubarak, saathi. Roz goliyan khilate ho, aaj dil bada karo, biryani khila dalo,' Satyapal told Javed one day, having checked the date on the frayed calendar hung inside his bunker, to find that it was Eid.

'Aaj Eid-e-Milad hai, saathi. Biryani nahi seviyan banayi jaati hain,' Javed responded good-naturedly. 'Kabhi hamare gaon aaiyega toh apni begum ke haath ki bani khilwayenge. Ungliyan chaat tey reh jaenge.'

'Haan, haan, kyun nahin. Pakka aaunga,' Satyapal answered back, at which Javed broke into a sher from Ghalib, who, as he had told Satyapal, was his favourite poet. 'Tire vaade par jiye ham toh ye jaan jhooth jaanaa, ki khushi se mar na jaate agar aitbaar hota.' Satyapal had vaguely heard of a television serial called *Mirza Ghalib*, but he had absolutely no idea who the man was. And he wasn't particularly interested.

'Insha Allah, Diwali mubarak ho, saathi. We are waiting for the fireworks,' Javed told Satyapal on Diwali.

'Oh yes! You guys had better be careful,' Satyapal answered back cheekily. 'We'll make sure our rockets target your post.'

'Miyan! You think we don't have firecrackers? If you people want your butts safe, make sure you don't step out of your bunker. We are the ones sitting on higher ground. We will set your tails on fire,' Javed responded. His deep, throaty chuckle rang out across the icy landscape and Satyapal, too, smiled.

* * *

At the highest battlefield of the world, the two enemies had become each other's emotional support. Javed often spoke to Satyapal about the baby daughter he had not yet seen. 'If I stay alive, I will go back and see her. Shabana likhti hain hamare jaisi aankhen hai unki,' he told Satyapal.

'Kaisi aankhen hain aapki?' a curious Satyapal asked. Even if he looked through his binoculars he could not see Javed's eyes, or even his face for that matter; he only knew his slightly raspy voice and his loud, open laughter.

'Badi aur bhoori,' Javed answered back, proudly.

'Aishwarya Rai jaisi?' Satyapal wanted to know.

'Arre nahi, bhai. Aishwarya ki toh hari hain. Hamari bhoori. Brown,' Javed retorted.

'Aah! Like Rani Mukherjee. Lovely!' Satyapal sighed. 'Your daughter could become a film star too . . .'

But Javed cut him short. 'Bilkul nahi. Padha likha ke daktar banayenge.'

Satyapal, too, had told Javed about his old, retired, soldier father, who had insisted that he, Satyapal, join the army. 'I never wanted to be a soldier but I wasn't good at studies, so Bauji took me to Kotdwar for the recruitment rally. I ran like the wind and came in the first five, but I got rejected for my hearing,' he confided honestly in Javed. 'Bauji spoke to a brigadier sahab he had served with. We got a minor surgery done and I was selected.'

He told Javed that his marriage had been fixed for December. The girl was from a neighbouring village. He hadn't seen her yet, but Bauji had written in his last letter that she was eighth-fail, fair and slim. 'Kheti ka kaam jaanti hai. Maa ki madad ho jaayegi,' he said.

Javed wanted to know if she would always stay in the village with his parents. 'Won't she come to live with you in the cantonment?' he asked.

Satyapal wasn't sure. 'I don't know about that, saathi,' he answered. 'Puchha nahi hai Bauji se.'

'Never mind. You will get to see her when you go home on leave. The army never gives you time during duty hours anyway,' Javed told him. 'Pahadi girls are very pretty. I am sure your begum is beautiful too,' he said warmly, making Satyapal grin from ear to ear.

Only recently, Satyapal had shared a secret fear with Javed. He said that the glacier scared him. The tall peaks all around suffocated him. He wanted to go back home to the lush green hills and the wide, open, yellow mustard fields of Tehri Garhwal, but he had no choice. 'Mujhe barf mein dab ke mar jaane se bahut dar lagta hai, saathi,' he told Javed. 'Even since I got locked in our dark and dingy cattle shed in the village in childhood, I have always been claustrophobic. That is why I always ask Sahab to put me on guard duty. Sitting inside that small, dark hut suffocates me. Mera dam ghut ta hai andar.'

'Arre! Never forget that your mind is free, saathi. Next time you feel afraid, close your eyes and think about the pretty Pahadi girl who will soon be your begum,' Javed advised him. 'One day we shall all die. Why worry about it every day? Maut ka ek din muayyan hai, neend kyun raat bhar nahi aati.' Javed was probably quoting Ghalib again. Satyapal had already started fantasizing about his wife-to-be, which wasn't easy since he had never seen her.

* * *

One morning, Satyapal told Javed that he would not be on guard duty the next day. He and Rifleman Ramesh had been detailed for a routine check of communication lines. Every ten days, three soldiers were sent to check the wires that kept the telephone connection, between the post and the company headquarters about two kilometres away, running. The post and the HQ each had the responsibility to maintain 1 km of the communication line—to ensure the wires were intact and working, not broken or buried in the snow. Since their very lives depended on it, the soldiers carried out the task with complete sincerity.

The empty jerry cans that had been used to cart kerosene to the post were put to good use here. They were filled with snow, which would quickly freeze into hard ice. The heavy jerry cans were then used as support for the telephone lines, which were tied on top of them, so that the wires would not get buried after heavy snowfall.

'We plan to leave by 8 a.m. and return before noon,' Satyapal told Javed, who nodded. Every soldier on Siachen knew that the weather usually turned late afternoon, so all activities were planned in such a way that the soldiers would be back in their bunkers by lunchtime.

Javed had received a letter, brought by a new soldier reporting on duty from leave. His daughter was unwell, he told Satyapal. 'I can't do anything for them from here. I feel so helpless,' he said. He sounded sad that morning.

'Don't worry, saathi, she will be fine. Children keep falling sick all the time,' Satyapal consoled him. Soon after, Satyapal told Javed he would now see him after a day.

'Khuda hafiz, saathi,' Javed called out to him. 'Apna khayal rakhna.'

'You too, Javed Bhai. And don't worry so much about your daughter. I am sure she is absolutely fine by now,' Satyapal reassured him and, with a casual wave of his hand, stepped inside his bunker.

* * *

The next afternoon, a sudden avalanche took the soldiers by surprise. Icy winds screamed outside their huts, as they huddled together inside their bunkers, drawing comfort from each other's presence and from the warmth of the kerosene stove.

Around 2 p.m., Javed was in his sleeping bag, rereading his wife's letter. Omar, the designated cook for the week, was cooking rice to go with the meat tins they planned to open for lunch. Their four other soldier comrades were playing cards, and radio operator Rifleman Faizal Sharief, quiet and withdrawn by temperament, was, as always, sitting in a corner by himself, listening to Skardu Radio. 'Do Hindustani sipahi Siachen Glacier ki Rana Post mein baraf ke neeche zinda dafan,' the newsreader was saying. None of the soldiers was paying attention to the news but the moment they heard Siachen mentioned they all started listening.

'Aawaaz unchi kar, Faizal,' Javed called out, placing the letter under his pillow.

The woman reading the news in her crisp Urdu was not giving many details, but she clearly stated that three Indian soldiers had been caught in an avalanche that afternoon. While one had been found, two were reported missing, presumed buried in the snowpack created by the avalanche.

For a moment there was abject silence in the bunker. Then, one of the card players spoke: 'So we have two less enemy soldiers to fight. The glacier got to the bastards before we did. Achhi khabar hai. Miyan, tum patte baanto.'

The four of them chuckled loudly and got back to their game. They did not notice the disquiet that shadowed Javed's face, but Faizal was watching him thoughtfully. 'Apne niche wali post ke bande lagte hain,' he said to

Javed. 'Isn't that Rana Post? Javed bhai aap toh baat karte ho na unmein se ek se?' Faizal sounded concerned. Javed just nodded.

Javed remembered that Satyapal had to go and check the communication lines that day and desperately hoped that he was not among the men missing.

* * *

Faizal spent the afternoon intercepting radio messages from the Indian side, with Javed sitting next to him. There were frequent references to the two missing soldiers. Four soldiers from the HQ and four from Rana Post had been sent to search for them. Repeated instructions were being passed on to the search party to step carefully, to avoid the edges of precipices, rendered indistinct by the freshly fallen snow.

'We don't know where to look, sahab,' the helpless JCO-in-charge was telling the young officer based at Rana Post, whom Javed knew from references in Satyapal's conversations. 'Nearly three feet of snow has fallen and the area is as expansive as a football field. It's like looking for a needle in a haystack.'

The search party had been told to divide the route and do a systematic search using metal poles to dig deep into the snow every two feet. 'If you feel a body, start digging,' the young Captain's voice conveyed urgency. 'Time bahut kam hai. We can't let them die, sahab,' he was telling the

JCO-in-charge. Javed knew that the Indian Army never deserted its men and was very hopeful that the two would be found.

That evening, when he knelt down and bent his head for namaz, Javed prayed for his friend. 'Allah! Please let him go back to his family,' Javed mumbled under his breath, still on his knees, head bent in a sajda. But when night fell and the rescue operation was suspended till next morning, he started losing hope. Surviving a night in the open on the glacier was very difficult.

* * *

Javed could hardly sleep the whole night, while the wind raged outside their hut in the darkness, screaming at them for trespassing in space meant only for nature at its most furious. His mind kept taking him back to the young boy from a small village in India, who was scared of closed spaces, whose nikah had been fixed with a girl he had never seen, who had been his emotional support all these days.

He imagined Satyapal buried under layers of snow that must slowly be hardening into ice. He hoped Satyapal was thinking about the beautiful girl his marriage had been fixed to and not about the barn he got locked in as a child. He desperately hoped his friend would hang on to life till the rescue operation was resumed in the morning.

When he awoke, dawn was breaking. His head heavy with lack of sleep, he woke Faizal up and asked him to switch on the radio set. Indian soldiers had resumed the search at first light. 'These people just don't leave their comrades,' Faizal muttered admiringly.

Javed stepped out to perform his morning chore, a mug of hot water in his hands. When he returned, the other soldiers were still sleeping. Faizal had a grim look on his face. 'They found the bodies, Javed Bhai,' he said softly. 'Both had frozen to death.'

Javed still nursed a faint hope. 'Did they give names?' he asked, his heart beating with anxiety.

'Yes. Ramesh Kumar and Satyapal,' Faizal replied. Tears streamed down Javed's face even as Faizal watched, quickly averting his eyes to let him grieve in dignity.

* * *

For many days after that, Javed opted out of sentry duty. He would sometimes cook for his comrades. Sometimes he would look after maintenance, but he could not gather the courage to go out of the bunker and look at the Indian post. Those days, he hardly ate and mostly kept to himself, grieving in solitude for the friend he had lost. He would read the Quran every day. On most nights he would toss around in his sleeping bag, waking up in the morning to find his pillow moist.

His thoughts would keep taking him back to the day of the avalanche. He would think of the cold, unforgiving ice that had suffocated Satyapal to a painful death. He would hear Satyapal screaming for help. Screams that could never escape that coffin of ice he had been trapped in. He prayed that Satyapal had died quickly without suffering too much. He hoped Satyapal's last thoughts had been not of death but of the bright-yellow mustard fields in his village.

Then one morning, after nearly a month, Javed decided to go back to his sentry duty. He slipped his legs into his snowsuit, zipping it up over his woolen tights and vest. Putting on his snow shoes, he reached for his woolen cap. He wore his glasses and pushed his fingers into the insulation gloves. Then, slipping his AK-47 over his shoulder, he stepped out of the fibre-glass hut. It was a pleasant morning, the sun was up, but as he stood in the icy wilderness he felt sad and completely alone for the first time in many days.

Thinking about the friend he had never really seen but had now lost, he looked towards the Indian side. Another sentry stood there. He was covered from head to toe in the familiar bhaloo suit. Javed turned his head to look far into the distance, blinking back tears.

And then, an unfamiliar voice rang out: 'Saathi!'

The soldier on guard duty outside the Indian post was calling out to him. Javed ignored him completely.

'Walekum salaam, saathi. Sania Mirza ko wapis nahi maangenge. Baat toh kar lo hamse.' Javed could sense a smile in the Indian soldier's voice.

He wiped off the tears freezing on his cheeks with the back of his glove and raised his arm to wave a greeting back at the nameless, faceless enemy.

Insomnia

The voices were back. He could hear them in the dark. 'Mat maaro sa'ab. Hamara koi kasoor nahi. Woh hamein gaon se utha kar le gaye the.' The Kashmiri accent was unmistakable. It suggested youth, the bulge of a newly sprouted Adam's apple, the rush of a shikara splashing through the water lilies in the Jhelum (or 'Jehe-lam', as the Kashmiris pronounced it). It was uncanny how clearly he remembered that face even after all these years. The razor-sharp nose, the translucent skin, the grey eyes flecked with green. He could even remember the faded blue check of his crushed shirt, the top button open, his neck showing where his phiran had fallen loose. It was an image as clear as crystal.

And then his wife cribbed that he was getting Alzheimer's. Just because he sometimes couldn't recollect where he had placed the car keys or the stick they used to chase monkeys out of their vegetable garden. What an insufferable nag she had become. It was a relief that she was sleeping in the other bedroom these days (his frequent trips

to the toilet disturbed her sleep, she said). And that was
fine with him. He preferred being by himself.

* * *

The General switched on his reading lamp and stretched
his hand, fumbling for the alarm clock. He pressed
the tab at the top, lighting up the screen. 0130 hours.
Swearing under his breath, he shut his eyes and let his
head drop back on the pillows. What he would give for
just one night of undisturbed sleep! It was something he
had been pining for ever since he retired from service,
more than fifteen years ago. But these Kashmiri bastards
wouldn't let that happen. He lifted his Alprax-heavy
head from the pillow, lowered his feet to the floor, his
toes sinking into the namda rug by his bedside. The
General rose slowly, put on his slippers and made his
way to the bathroom, his knees stiff from having been
stretched out for so long.

The moment he flushed the toilet, he regretted it. His
wife was a light sleeper. She would hear the water gushing
and realize he was up. She would crib about it the next
morning, making him feel guilty about disrupting her
sleep. He stood still for a moment and listened. There was
no sound from her bedroom. But he knew that his hearing
was not what it used to be. (Which was also a blessing
in some ways—he could no longer hear her retarded TV
serials.) He carefully closed the toilet door, ensuring that

it did not bang shut, and shuffled back to the bed. For a while, he sat with his legs dangling over its side. Then, pulling his feet up, he drew the fleece blanket to his chest, switched the lamp off and lay in the dark with his eyes shut, willing himself to fall asleep again.

A dry, raspy cough broke the stillness of the night. The General's eyes flew open. It was the old man this time, his voice hoarse from fatigue, begging for the boy's life: 'Mat maaro sa'ab. Bachcha hai. Aapko dua dega.' He knew there were five of them. Standing outside his bedroom window every night, the darkness seeping into their dirty, frayed phirans, which had holes burnt into them by the embers of the kangdis that had kept them alive in sub-zero temperatures. Tired, unwashed, starving. Sobbing, pleading, motherfucking bastards. Waking him up from rum-induced sleep to beg for their miserable lives. Fifty years had passed but they hadn't stopped whining in his ears.

The General's mind travelled. He could feel the chill of Kashmir turning his nose red, the snug wrap of his thick Denison smock, the reassuring grip of his old green helmet with that little rip in the lining where the cold metal pressed against his scalp. And the smell. The smell of smoking pinewood mingled with the stench of unwashed clothes. And garlic. That insufferable bloody garlic. He had definitely smelt it on the boy's breath. The starving rat had been chewing garlic. Where the fuck had he managed to get garlic from on that barren peak? The smell was so nauseating that he had to turn his head and grope for a cigarette.

* * *

On his previous visit to the hospital, a grim-looking respiratory specialist had told him to throw away his cigarettes and not buy another packet ever if he wanted to live. 'You have damaged a large portion of your lungs by chain-smoking, sir. If you continue, they will just collapse.' The General had guessed it already. There was a time when he loved walking. Now, he took the car everywhere. To the market, the bank, the barber, when he went to pay the electricity bill or visit the Ex-servicemen League, where he did some voluntary work, sorting out pension and land issues for retired soldiers. He could no longer walk without getting breathless.

The cough returned each morning. And lately (he hadn't told his wife though) he had been spitting blood into the bathroom sink. The first day he saw that blob of red on the white ceramic, he froze, and groped around in his mouth to see if he had cut his gums while brushing his teeth. He hadn't. The blood came from inside. It collected in an uncomfortable mass in his throat, constricting his food passage, and when he coughed hard it came up, leaving a salty, metallic taste on his tongue that no amount of rinsing could take away. Soon it became an everyday occurrence, and he got used to handling it. He would turn on the tap, rub the ominous red stains on the basin with his wet fingers and wash them away. He had read that end-stage COPD was like drowning. Patients would suffocate to a painful death. But he didn't care. He preferred to die breathing in the sweetness of nicotine rather than smell the garlic on that Kashmiri bastard's breath.

* * *

'Sa'ab zee. Sa'ab zee. O sa'ab!' The whispers were getting louder. They had walked up to the wire mesh on the window; their faces hidden in the shadows of the shawls draped around their heads and shoulders. They were reciting the Quran now. The General was feeling compelled to pull the curtain, press his nose against the glass and look out, but he stopped himself. He had done it before so many times. There was never anyone there. Just abject darkness and the droopy outline of the Alphonso mango tree that had grown from a sapling his daughter had sent him from Ratnagiri many years back. He looked at his double-barrel rifle, with a piece of cotton stuffed down its nozzle, propped against the wall behind the door. It had been with him longer than his kids. Or even his wife. He looked at it with tenderness. It had been years since he held it but his fingers remembered its reassuring feel. One day, he promised himself that he would open the window, call out to the bastards and when they showed their dirty, stinking faces from behind the hedge, where he knew they hid each night, he would shoot them in their bloody heads.

* * *

Fifty years back . . . There were five of them. Grey dots in the distance. Almost blending in with the landscape. It was the movement that had given them away. If the motherfuckers had stayed still, he would have never realized they were hiding there. But they hadn't. So he knew. And they knew that he knew.

A strange cat-and-mouse game was unfolding on the rocky terrain of Gurez. Looking through his binoculars, a smoking cigarette dangling between his fingers, the Major could figure out that the rebels were trying to use the rocks to shelter themselves from the cold winds. He could make out the outlines of their guns against the jagged cliffs. Spanking new AK-47s. Handed over to young boys who had been bribed or bullied to die in a meaningless war no one wanted to fight any more. Not the villagers, not the Pakistanis, not the Indian Army. And least of all, him. He was tired and frustrated and only interested in staying alive, so he could get back home to his wife and newborn daughter, whom he hadn't even seen yet. His wife had promised to get a photograph taken of the child and send it in her next letter. He could hardly wait. 'She has a nose like yours,' she had written. 'And when she smiles, she gets a dimple in the left cheek. Just like you do.' He doubted if all that would show in a picture. If only he could get some leave, he would go home and see her. Take her in his arms. Kiss her forehead. Hold her close to his heart. But there was so much militancy in his area these days that he knew there was no chance of that happening in the next few months. He wasn't even sure if he would stay alive to see her at all.

The Kashmir posting was a bloody curse. A bleeding cross on the shoulder that could not be put down; it could only change hands. He would be free when another unfortunate officer replaced him and began his own two-year walk on the edge of hell. The Major didn't care if a nuclear bomb dropped on Kashmir that very night. He hated these squealing pigs that lived on government grants and double-crossed the soldiers who courted death to make their lives safe. He hated them as much as he hated the politicians responsible for the mess they were all in. Any idiot knew that keeping Kashmir burning helped take attention away from national issues that really mattered. So many young soldiers were killed every year. Young, motivated boys who were ready to give their lives for their country were brought back home in body bags that whipped up national hysteria for a short while, and then things got back to where they always stood, frozen in time. It was a wicked, filthy, ghastly war in which the enemy never came face to face but stayed undercover and used remotely operated IED bombs that blew up convoys and left soldiers without limbs and life.

He spat out the saliva building up in his mouth with an angry snarl.

'Climb down and walk to us with your hands in the air. We will spare your lives,' he shouted once again, his voice carrying in the wind. 'Surrender and you shall be given government protection. This is my promise to you.' The armed rebels were surrounded and outnumbered. They didn't really have a choice. The Major had no intention of taking his men up the mountain if he could avoid it. Though there were just five rebels, they had the advantage of height. They could see who was coming up and could shoot to kill. He was not going to let a single soldier die if he could help it. They were his comrades, ready to unquestioningly follow his command. He felt responsible for their lives.

That was why his company had been sitting there quietly for more than forty-eight hours, watching. Like cats waiting for mice. The Major lit another cigarette and squinted in the orange glow of the setting sun. The night was going to be tricky. He would not be able to track their movements after dark. He had to convince them to come to him before that.

* * *

'Daro mat. Maine apne seniors se baat kar li hai. If you surrender to me, you will not be harmed. Aapko surrendered militants ki tarah treat kiya jayega. Rehabilitation hoga. Naukri milegi. Your identity will be kept secret,' his voice echoed in the stillness of the falling dusk, conveying, he hoped, authority and kindness. And he hoped as hell that the fucking assholes could hear him clearly.

He repeated the message one more time, his voice beginning to crack from all the shouting. He trained his binoculars on the peak but could see nothing. 'I'd like a mug of hot tea. And you could also have food distributed to the soldiers. If they don't come down on their own, we will have to climb up,' he told his Company Junior Commissioned Officer, the efficient and dependable Subedar Durjan Singh. The Major leaned back on a boulder and closed his weary eyes.

'Sahab! It looks like they are descending,' Durjan Singh suddenly exclaimed. The Major got up with a start and asked for his binoculars. Durjan was right. They were indeed making their way down, rifles slung across their backs, arms swinging by their sides, executing that curious sideways jump walk that all Pahadis were adept at while coming down slopes. They were as sure-footed as mountain goats. It was obvious that this barren landscape was home to them. He watched narrow-eyed. As they came closer, he could see the naked fear on their faces. His soldiers had their guns trained at them.

'Walekum salaam,' he said to the old man leading the group. With his frizzy white beard, deep-set eyes, wrinkled face, phiran and skullcap, he could have been a learned maulvi. The Major's guess was that he was a handler. His job was to convince young men to turn into human bombs, strap themselves with explosives, blow themselves up in cantonments or marketplaces, drive RDX-loaded cars into army trucks. He would never risk his own life but had probably assured them that they were doing it all for divine justice and would be rewarded with jannat and virgins as gifts in the afterlife. The Major could see why the man inspired trust. His face was calm, his gaze steady. The rest of the group consisted of young boys, barely out of their teens. Thin, with grubby faces and smelly clothes, trembling in fear. Not hardened militants yet. But starting on that terrible journey that would lead to death and destruction.

The Major was polite but curt. He made them drop their weapons and stand with their hands in the air. His men interrogated them for information they could give, which wasn't much. The boys said they had been hand-picked from their villages just six months back, taken across the border for weapons training, provided with guns and were being brought back into Kashmir for creating trouble.

He made them stand in a row and gestured to Durjan Singh to offer them water. They drank thirstily from cupped palms. Their cracked lips and sunken eyes were proof that they had been starving on the mountain. Lifting his rifle, the Major looked the old man in the eye and said, 'I'm sorry, but water is all I can give you.'

The old man's cataract-glazed eyes were accusing. 'Aapne zubaan di thi sa'ab. Aap apna vaada tod rahe hain. Ye galat hai,' he said.

The Major lowered his gaze, 'Tell me something, baba,' he asked. 'When you kill soldiers using IED devices, cars laden with explosives? Human bombs? Wo sahi hai?'

'Wo jihaad hai,' the old man answered and dropped to his knees, reciting verses from the Quran.

'Toh phir samajh lijiye ki ye mera jihaad hai,' the Major replied. 'If I let you people go today, that is what you will do to us one day.'

One of the boys had started to cry. 'Mat maariye sa'ab,' he was pleading, 'wo hamein gaon se utha kar le gaye the.'

'Close your eyes,' the Major ordered, his voice colder than the icy wind lashing their faces. Lifting his rifle, he shot the boy through his heart. Tall and fair with a sharp nose, the boy couldn't have been older than nineteen. His open eyes had turned glassy in death. They were a beautiful grey flecked with green. 'Fucker. Could have been a film star,' the Major said, looking away from the blood staining the earth.

Four more shots rang out through the barren valley. The soldier with the walkie-talkie connected the circuit and held the instrument out to him. 'Charlie tiger for sixteen,' the Major said, his voice clear and confident. 'Fidayeen attack intercepted. Militants refused to surrender. We have made a kill.'

* * *

'Sa'ab! O sa'ab!' The whispers were getting louder. They were inside the room now. He could smell the nauseating sweat on their skin. The General got up coughing and rummaged in his drawer for the box of red cartridges that lay between the woolen socks and underwear. It took him a while to cock his heavy 12-bore rifle after all these years. He had to hold it between his knees and use all his weight to click it open. He pulled out the piece of old cotton stuffed inside the barrel, opened the breech, pushed a cartridge in and held his loaded rifle, feeling its familiar weight on his forearms. It filled him with deadly calm. He had done this so many times before.

The boy was touching him now. He had started shaking him by the shoulders. It was the garlic on his breath that the General couldn't stand any more. He lifted his rifle and pressed the trigger.

His wife lay at his feet. A pool of red was slowly spreading around her, seeping into the off-white edge of the namda on the floor. Beside her were shards of shattered glass and some spilt water. Her head was still covered by her shawl. Her lifeless hand held his strip of Alprax.

The General continued to sit on the edge of his bed and stared at her for what seemed like fifty years. He then dipped a trembling hand into the box by his side. Putting all his weight on the barrel, he snapped the breech block open to push a cartridge in one last time.

13 Para Goes to South Glacier

'So this is bloody Chalunka!' exclaimed Major Somnath Batabyal. With hands still on the steering wheel of his just parked army jeep, he was staring gloomily at the claustrophobic cluster of bare brown mountains before him. Known by his nickname 'Bat Ball' in the unit, Batabyal had driven two days from Leh—along with the 13 Para main body—crossing the famous Khardung La pass at 17,000 feet, where he had seen snow for the first time in his life, and after a night halt at a midway transit camp, he had finally arrived at the unit's new destination. Chalunka was the regimental headquarters from where they would soon be deployed on South Glacier, considered one of the toughest postings in the Indian Army.

The Commanding Officer of the unit, Colonel Jang Bir Singh, Vir Chakra, had reached Chalunka a few days back for a formal taking over from the outgoing 38 JAK RIF, a highly respected and pompous hundred-year-old unit that kept its nose up in the air because of its exquisite lineage, which had given the country two Army Chiefs and the legendary General Zordar Singh, Victoria Cross, who had left the planet many years ago but continued to glower down from photographs at almost all army establishments.

A short, slim guy in combat dress, with a bushy moustache and big teeth, jumped out of the passenger seat of Bat Ball's jeep.

'Jannat! I love it,' he declared, surveying the desolate scenery through a snazzy pair of gold-rimmed Aviator shades. Co-driver to Bat Ball, Major Navrang Apte had an appetite for extreme discomfort and lived by his own motto, which was: the colder the better; the wetter the better; the hotter the better. 'Bahar nikal, chutiye,' he directed a piercing jibe at Bat Ball. 'Your Junior Command course at Mhow has made you a sissy. Aur grade bhi kya leke aaya hai—alpha. Shameful! Real soldiers always get charlie grading. They don't believe in this academic nonsense,' he declared, gleefully rubbing his hands.

The latest addition to the unit, Lt Gurbachan Singh, a Sword of Honour recipient from the Indian Military Academy, on his first posting, had joined the rest of the team at Leh. He emerged from the back of the jeep and stood next to Apte, towering over his five feet five inches with his own six-five height, plus a few inches of turban.

'Look bachche! This is your home now,' Apte said to Singh, at which the gigantic bachcha nodded obediently.

By then, another jeep had screeched to a noisy halt beside them, spilling out its contents—the remaining officer strength of 13 Para: Unit Resident Medical Officer,

Dr Capt. Gurpreet Grewal (Garry), whose spectacled eyes had been glinting with excitement ever since he had heard that the unit was going to South Glacier; and the driver of the jeep, the handsome, clean-shaven Coorgi, Maj. G.N. Cariappa (Carie), who liked to scowl darkly at the world at all times and was, at the moment, scowling darkly at the mountains of Chalunka.

Three olive-green Shaktiman trucks carrying the rest of the unit were slowly winding their way in, with curious soldiers sticking their heads out to get a first view of their new location, anticipating the chai, pakoda, halwa party organized for them by the outgoing unit as per tradition.

Keen-eyed Apte had spotted the duty sentry in the distance who was making his way towards them. 'Lamba kadam rakh! Oye!' he yelled, making the sentry jump and break into a sprint. 'Beta, at that speed you would have reached us tomorrow,' he patiently explained to the out-of-breath soldier, adding a 'shabash' when the sentry pointed out the officers' quarters to him.

The officers' accommodation appeared to be a quaint-looking barrack of five single rooms with a common corridor, which the officers unanimously decided to visit and investigate. Each room had walls built almost entirely of stacked empty jerry cans, bound in cement, which had once been used to deliver kerosene to Chalunka. An asbestos sheet stretched and nailed on top served as the roof.

A soldier stood outside the barrack, heating water in a tin can on a kerosene stove. 'Oye shabash!' Apte declared, whistling in appreciation. Stepping inside the first room, he looked up to find a parachute stretched across the roof as a sort of thermal insulation against the cold asbestos sheet. 'By god ki kasam, a parachute here too?' he exclaimed.

'Abey saale, you are a paratrooper. Ye parachute teri maa hai. You'd be dead if it wasn't around,' snapped Carie, coming up from behind him, lugging a big rucksack.

Apte looked back at him seriously. 'Sir, I'm not sure I want my mom watching me from the roof of my room,' he replied, folding his hands in a pranam and mouthing a 'Namaste Mataji' to the parachute even as Carie kicked him from behind.

Dumping their backpacks on the groundsheet-covered floor, the two of them lay stretched on the twin beds inside the hut. Bat Ball, too, had arrived by then. Poking his head in, he let out a loud, 'Oh bhen . . .' when Carie cut him short.

'Mind your language, bugger. You are in the presence of a senior officer,' Carie said, at which Bat Ball burst into a string of expletives.

'I'll have you locked up in the quarter guard one of these days.' Carie grinned. 'Come sit down. Let's play cards till the chai arrives.' He whipped out a pack of cards from the big pocket of his dungarees.

An alarmed-looking Gurbachan arrived at the quarters carrying his large black box, marked 'Indian Military

Academy', with the help of the jeep driver. Having peeped inside the first room, he hastily moved on to the next one before he could be noticed.

Carie positioned his head more comfortably on the pillow and started dealing the cards with practised ease.

* * *

An hour later, chai and halwa arrived and were devoured. After burping their approval, the paratroopers began their third round of cards. Apte had attached his Walkman to a speaker, playing some sad Manna Dey numbers and tunelessly whistling along to them. Garry was stretched out on the floor, with his head resting on his backpack, deeply engrossed in a Frederick Forsyth novel he had picked up from Modern Book Store in Agra just before the move. In short, all was perfect with their world, which was probably why the boys did not notice the ominous tread of heavy DMS boots outside.

The tin door to the hut was pushed open and a dark face—nearly twice the size of what's considered average in Homo sapiens, with a handlebar moustache, bushy eyebrows, dark eyes and a snarl on the lip—poked inside.

'You bloody assholes! Shut off that bloody radio,' the booming voice of their Commanding Officer Colonel Jang Bir Singh, lovingly called Krur Singh behind his back, shattered the moment of peace inside the tent. Carie jumped off the bed, sending the cards in his hand flying.

Bat Ball, who had been leaning on the bedside, sprang to attention. Apte fell on top of his beloved Walkman in his hurry to turn it off. And a startled Garry, executing a perfect paratrooper's landing roll—distributing shock sequentially along the balls of feet, sides of calves, thighs, hips and back—disappeared under the bed.

Crawling out with his book still in his hands, Garry saw that Carie had, by then, jumped to the CO's side and was respectfully holding the door open for him with a polite 'Good evening, sir.'

'Why didn't one of you morons report to me after reaching the location?' Krur Singh thundered. 'And why are you bloody chaps still lying around, you shammers! Get ready. We have been invited to dinner by the outgoing unit. We leave at 7.45 p.m.'

All four officers clicked their heels together and uttered a crisp 'Yes, sir!' at which a satisfied-looking Krur Singh turned around, puffed up his chest to its impressive fifty-six-inch girth, brushed some imaginary dust off his combat uniform and left the hut with a smirk on his face.

'Old man is going to giving me a heart attack one of these days,' Bat Ball declared, wiping beads of sweat off his brow. 'For his mammoth size, his stealth moves are really smooth.'

'Saale, how do you think he got his Vir Chakra?' Apte asked, starting to deal the cards. 'He sneaked up weaponless on a Pakistani post and shouted at them so loudly that they all had heart attacks and died.' They both broke into a chuckle.

'Shut up, you idiots. Don't joke about a gallantry award,' Carie snapped at them.

'Sir, but what are we going to wear to dinner?' Garry asked, in an attempt to change the topic.

'Bugger! It's a field location. We will go in our combats,' Carie replied. The boys didn't really have much of a choice. Since Carie had already done a field posting in Nagaland, under his able guidance they had all packed just two uniforms, four combats, underwear, boots, socks, shaving kits, etc., in their backpacks and had added a pair of jeans and a few T-shirts, thinking they would check out the Leh Market if they got a chance. 'We are off to war, buggers. You don't need pansy clothes,' Carie had told them.

Feeling relaxed, the three returned to their game. Garry placed his book on his chest, closed his eyes and started to snore gently.

* * *

At 7.30 p.m. sharp, fumes of an exotic perfume filled the hut, making Bat Ball wrinkle his nose and say, 'Who the hell farted?' He hadn't finished his sentence when in stepped an apparition that could have easily passed for a men's formal-wear supermodel. It was Krur Singh, dressed in his Sunday best. He was wearing an immaculate dark-grey three-piece suit, the blazer fitting perfectly around his broad shoulders. It was beautifully set off by a starched white shirt and a maroon Para tie. A shining Para brooch gleamed from his lapel, and silver cufflinks winked on his shirtsleeves. His black brogue shoes were sparkling like twin mirrors.

An involuntary and unintentionally disrespectful 'Oh teri!' escaped the mouth of the just-woken-up Garry, and he hastily tried to disguise it as a cough.

While the paratroopers gaped in wonder and astonishment at him, Krur Singh was obviously not reciprocating their sentiments. 'You bloody pigs!' he snarled at the shabbily dressed, dirty bunch in front of him. Once again, the cards went flying out of Carie's hands.

'A hundred-year-old, highly respected battalion has invited you for dinner. Is this how you plan to show up? In fifteen minutes flat, by my watch, I want you jokers lined up in front of my Jonga decently dressed. And each of you bloody chaps has to be in a tie.' He then turned around and was gone, leaving behind the heady scent of his perfume and a tense silence.

'He was wearing ma'am's Chanel No. 5,' Garry declared.

'Tu bada connoisseur hai perfumes ka. Shut up!' Carie scowled at him.

'Meri mummy lagaati hain,' Garry mumbled. 'I swear. I can identify it.'

Apte threw a pillow at him. There was a mad scramble as the officers emptied their rucksacks and hunted for decent clothes, of which they had none.

A thought suddenly flashed into Apte's wicked mind. 'Saala, Gurbachan,' he exclaimed. 'The bugger has come straight from the Academy. Tie ki puri dukaan hoga wo.'

He made quick work of getting to Gurbachan's room, followed closely by Bat Ball. Dressed in well-fitted trousers and an Academy blazer, Gurbachan was in the process of slipping his large feet into a pair of neatly polished shoes. Hearing of his seniors' predicament, he displayed a spirit of regimental camaraderie; and immediately spread out his collection of ties and formal clothes for them to choose from.

* * *

Fifteen minutes later, faces washed and hair combed, all five paratroopers lined up for inspection in front of the CO's Jonga at the parking lot. Krur Singh stepped out as though to a drum roll, resplendent in his suit. There was an angry intake of breath as his eyes took in the lot standing at attention before him, nervousness writ large on their faces.

The curly-haired Bat Ball had managed to get into Gurbachan's clothes. The trouser legs had been rolled up to make them a few inches shorter; the shirt was properly buttoned at the wrist, but both sleeves hung halfway down his palms. His uniform belt magnificently held the outfit together at the waist, with an elegant black tie knotted perfectly at his throat.

Garry was in his combat trousers. He had tucked into these Gurbachan's crisp white shirt and was proudly sporting a bright yellow tie with red polka dots on it.

Apte had dug out of his rucksack an olive-green Angola shirt, teaming it up with uniform pants and DMS boots. He was wearing the striped maroon-and-white Para tie, which he felt made a fine contrast against the green.

Carie, who had not been able to fit into any of Gurbachan's trousers, was in his own jeans and a red T-shirt. Gurbachan's oversized Indian Military Academy blazer and tie gave his outfit the desired air of formality.

Gurbachan himself was perfectly attired and standing a little away from the rest, as if trying to distance himself from his seniors.

'You,' Krur Singh said, pointing to Gurbachan, 'get inside my Jonga.' And then, turning to the rest of the sloppy-looking gang, he contemptuously spat out, 'Follow me in the jeep.'

Lance Naik Sartaj Singh, driver of the CO's Jonga, claimed at breakfast in the langar next morning, swearing upon his mother, that he actually saw coils of smoke emerging from CO Sahab's ears that evening.

* * *

The 38 JAK RIF field mess turned out to be nearly thirteen times grander than 13 Para's peacetime mess in Agra. The paratroopers beheld, open-mouthed, the teakwood furniture and silk carpets; the magnificent paintings of the two Army Chiefs and of General Zordar Singh, Victoria Cross, glaring at guests from the walls; the fountains spouting at the bar; the officers' wives (who happened to be visiting during the summer vacation) in the most exquisite saris; and the officers themselves in immaculate combinations and suits, with perfectly folded matching red silk kerchiefs in their coat pockets.

Other than one moment of weakness, when the 38 JAK RIF Commanding Officer Col Meherbaan Singh Shekhawat's stately moustache quivered while he took a first look at the boys of 13 Para lining up for a handshake, the unit lived up to its formidable reputation. From officers to ladies to waiters, every single person completely ignored the fancy dress four of their guests had turned up in, treating them with the utmost charm and courtesy. Krur Singh was the only one who refused to look at or talk to any of his officers until after dessert was served and goodnights were bid.

As they prepared to leave, he surprised the badly dressed bunch by brusquely inviting them to ride with him in his Jonga, ordering his driver to go back to the unit in the accompanying jeep. Opting to drive himself, he stared at an extremely nervous Carie seated next to him and burst into booming laughter.

'I am extremely sorry, sir. We let you down today,' Carie offered, looking suitably ashamed, with the others also chorusing an emotional 'Sorry, sir' from the back seat.

'You will let me down only if you don't perform in war, son. And I know you will never do that. My boys are not chocolate soldiers. We are fighting men. Forgiven and forgotten,' Krur Singh growled, his heart completely melted by the four large whiskies he'd had.

As the car screeched to a noisy stop outside the 13 Para mess, he ordered them to step out.

'Come on. Let's go have a Para peg in our own mess. These bloody JAK RIF guys make such bloody pansy drinks. And did you see those matching red rumaals in their pockets? Disgusting!' he spat out.

Though the night was dark, and according to Carie 'fucking butt-freezing cold', for the young paratroopers the birds had begun to sing, violins were playing and the sun shone brightly in the abject darkness, warming them right inside their hearts.

'Three cheers for Tiger!' Carie declared, the two large rums having made him bold. 'Hip hip hurray!' yelled the young paratroopers, slithering out of the CO's Jonga one after another.

Krur Singh, whistling a merry tune, put his arms around the shoulders of two of his boys as they all made their way to the bar, much to the dismay of the mess waiter who had only just called it a day. He knew it was going to be a long night.

The New Para Probationer

'Bhains ki aankh! Ye hai Lieutenant Mayank?' muttered a shocked Major Somnath Batabyal, Bravo Company Commander, his handsome face mirroring his disbelief.

'Sir, I think the army headquarters clerk drafting the signal missed an "a" at the end of the name,' offered his Company 2IC (second-in-command), the big-brained Captain Amit Dogra, or Doggy, who had his face hidden behind a copy of *Punjab Kesri*, which he was pretending to read.

The two of them stood at a roadside shack outside the Agra Cantt railway station. Batabyal, Bat Ball to his unit, was taking noisy swigs from a kulhar of masala chai.

Across the road from them was the object of their attention—a slim, fair girl in a demure salwar kameez, a thick plait hanging over one shoulder and her folded dupatta pinned at both sides. She was paying the coolie, who had deposited at her feet a black steel box that had 'Lt Mayanka Sharma, Officers Training Academy' stenciled on it in bold white letters. She had a knapsack on her back, from which she had earlier extracted her wallet and was now fishing out a cell phone.

Startled by his suddenly ringing cell, Bat Ball spilt some of his tea on Dogra, who yelped in pain. 'Sorry, man! Now stay quiet! It's her,' Bat Ball whispered and drawled 'Hello' into his phone.

'Good evening, sir. This is Lt Mayanka Sharma reporting. I have reached Agra, sir,' said the polite female voice at the other end.

'Welcome to the station, Mayanka. I hope you had a safe journey,' Bat Ball responded. 'I am sorry no vehicle could be detailed to pick you up because of a vehicle inspection tomorrow. I suggest you take a rickshaw and reach the 13 Para mess.'

'Right, sir. Good evening, sir,' Mayanka replied.

Bat Ball replaced his cell in his pocket and watched the girl across the road flagging down a passing cycle rickshaw. His hand involuntarily went to the large handlebar moustache glued to his face. It was borrowed from the Bravo Company Drama Party, who had been experts at creating disguises while the company operated incognito in Kashmir. He had also painted a large black mole on one cheek. Dogra had a thick layer of kajal in his eyes and was wearing a pair of bushy sideburns and a French beard. Both were dressed in glittery shirts, buttons open halfway to the waist; they had bought the shirts from a thela in Naulakha Bazaar. Doggy had tied a colourful handkerchief around his neck, while Bat Ball was wearing a shiny silver chain gifted to him by his sister on Rakhi.

The two of them were on a mission. They had been tasked with scaring the daylights out of the new Para probationer joining the unit, as per a decades-old tradition that had been a source of entertainment for all members of the battalion. Since they believed that the newcomer was a gentleman officer— the joining letter had mentioned the name 'Lt Mayank Sharma'—their plan was to not send a vehicle, follow the youngster on a bike, accost him on a dark street, flash a knife and take away his identity card and wallet. That was to be followed up by putting him in the quarter guard for a few hours as punishment for losing his ID card. Though Mayank having turned into a Mayanka had given them a bit of a jolt, the original plan was nevertheless to be carried out.

They watched Mayanka load her box on to the rickshaw and then climb up herself. Bat Ball paid for his tea and, turning the ignition key, brought his Bullet to a roaring start. 'Quick, get on, Doggy,' he said, 'let's not lose her in the crowd.' They started following the rickshaw as it zipped down the road, dodging cows, dogs and pedestrians at a high speed. 'Saala. He thinks he's Michael Schumacher,' Doggy said with a scowl. 'Ek thappad isko lagana padega.'

* * *

'She's barely five feet tall,' Bat Ball said to Doggy, who was leaning over his shoulder. 'Isko fauj mein liya kisne?'

'Sir, 152 centimetres is the required height for female candidates, that is 4.98 feet,' Doggy replied, showing off his GK and maths in one stroke. 'I think she just about made it.'

'Shakal se hi darpok lag rahi hai. I don't think you will need the knife. Just shout in her ear and she will get scared,' Bat Ball chortled, adding, 'Mark my words, Doggy, she will be out of here in fifteen days. No chance of her completing the Para probation.'

Doggy agreed wholeheartedly. 'Para is not for women in any case, sir. Or even for ordinary men. Only the toughest guys wear the maroon beret,' he haughtily declared, making both his and Bat Ball's chests swell a few inches.

As the rickshaw turned towards the dark road connecting Sadar Bazaar to the cantonment, where half the streetlights never worked, Bat Ball decided the location was perfect for their undercover operation. Speeding up, he brought the bike close to the rickshaw and started cruising alongside it. Then, deepening his voice to its lowest baritone, he growled, 'Oye rickshaw! Ruk saale.'

Alarmed by this, the rickshaw-puller started pedalling even faster. Doggy whipped out from his sling bag a long knife, whose blade glinted dangerously in the moonlight. 'Be careful with that knife,' Bat Ball mumbled. 'One scratch on her and Krur Singh will slit both our throats.'

The officers of 13 Para lived in mortal fear of their Commanding Officer, Colonel Jang Bir Singh, Vir Chakra, affectionately called Krur Singh (behind his back). Krur Singh did not mind probationers being ragged, but he had standing orders that they were not to be touched.

Doggy was warming up to his role. 'Rickshaw rok, saale. Nahi toh chakku ghusa dunga tere pet mein,' he growled. He heard the woman saying, 'Ruk jaiye, bhaiyaji,' at which the terrified rickshaw-puller braked reluctantly.

'Hand over your watch and wallet quietly, madam. We will not touch you,' Doggy snarled as Bat Ball moved ahead and blocked the rickshaw with his bike.

'We scared her. She's taking off her watch,' Doggy whispered to Bat Ball and, getting off the backseat, swaggered over to the rickshaw. He was surprised to see that Mayanka had handed over her watch to the scrawny rickshaw-puller and was now walking briskly towards him. Before he could realize what was happening, she jumped in the air and kicked him hard between the legs. With a piercing scream of pain, Doggy collapsed, sending his knife clattering on the road.

Mayanka moved fast. She picked up the knife, went towards Doggy and looked at him with undisguised fury. 'Saale chutiye!' she said, making both the rickshaw-puller and Bat Ball recoil. 'How dare you accost an officer of the Indian Army. Now wait and see what I do to you. First I shall break all your bones. Then I shall cut you into small small pieces,' she declared, supremely confident. She aimed another kick at Doggy even as Bat Ball leapt forward to his defence. He managed to grapple with Mayanka and wrestle the knife out of her hands. She had taken on a judo stance and Bat Ball barely saw the punch coming till it hit him straight in the eye. Her other elbow hit him hard in the ear, making him see an entire constellation of stars. 'Run!' he shouted at Doggy, flinging the knife into the bushes so as not to cut her accidentally.

Shielding his face from the blows being rained on it by the furious lady officer, Bat Ball sprinted towards his bike. She had grabbed his silver chain and was hanging on to it with a vice-like grip. 'I will teach you bastards a lesson you will never forget,' she said, thrusting her knee into Bat Ball's solar plexus, making him momentarily lose his breath. He pushed her hard, making her roll on the ground and quickly got on his bike. He revved up the engine as Doggy came limping and managed to straddle the bike.

From the corner of his eye, Doggy could see the desi version of Lara Croft rising to her feet and getting into attack mode once again, her long plait falling over a shoulder, eyes breathing fire, dupatta still pinned in its place. She came charging at them, but Bat Ball accelerated just in time and zoomed away. 'Darpok, gandu saale! Never fool around with a soldier ever again,' she was shouting.

Though moaning in pain, Doggy managed to whisper 'Sir, gaaliyan saari aati hain isko' in Bat Ball's ear, which was slowly turning red from the hard punch she had landed on it.

Lt Mayanka walked back to the rickshaw, wiping her hands on her kurta, and took her watch back from the rickshaw-puller, who was gaping at her in open-mouthed admiration. 'Thank you, bhaiyaji,' she said with a smile. 'Papaji ne di hai. Toot jaati toh bura maan jaate.'

* * *

That evening, Doggy could not make it to the dinner hosted in the 13 Para mess. He had been advised two days of bed rest by the unit's Resident Medical Officer. It was the first time in the regiment's history that Col Jang Bir Singh—he of the flashing dark eyes and lush moustache—who had been briefed about the thrashing Bat Ball and Doggy had received, did not scowl while shaking hands with a Para probationer. 'You need to be very tough to complete the probation,' he said, fixing Mayanka with his piercing gaze. 'Do you have it in you?'

'Yes, sir,' she replied, boldly meeting her Commanding Officer's eyes.

He smiled, said 'All the best' and moved on to greet the other guests.

Bat Ball was at the bar, nursing a large Old Monk (half paani, half soda), when the ramrod-straight, smartly dressed lady officer walked up to him. She was wearing grey trousers and a long-sleeved white shirt that covered the Band-Aids on her scraped elbows. Her hair was neatly tied up in a bun. 'Good evening, sir. Lt Mayanka Sharma,' she said, introducing herself.

'Major Somnath Batabyal.' He stood up, holding out his arm for a handshake. A purple bruise had spread around one of his eyes, scarring his dark, handsome face.

'Did you hurt yourself, sir?' she asked, looking concerned.

'Oh! Just a minor accident,' he replied airily and offered her a drink.

They sat on adjacent bar stools, drinking in silence for a while. And then, her slim-fingered hand slipped something over the counter to where he had placed his glass. 'I think you dropped this, sir,' she said softly and stood up to leave.

Bat Ball's silver chain winked up at him. It had snapped in one place. He picked it up, smiled and slipped it into his pocket.

* * *

Author's note: Women officers cannot join the Parachute Regiment at present. But one day they probably shall, and that is when someone like Lt Mayanka would come along and challenge misconceptions.

Déjà Vu

Major Sarah Varghese balanced the injection tray she was carrying in the crook of her arm and turned her wrist to check the time, only to realize that she had forgotten to wear her watch. Completing her final round of the wards for the day, she peered through the glass window of Room 12 in the children's section. A soft yellow glow lit the room.

Dakshina was turned to her side, writing something in her diary. The pink hard plastic cover could be locked with a tiny key that she wore around her neck on a leather string. Her two fat plaits hung below her shoulders. Her fractured leg was wrapped in what was once white plaster but now looked like a colourful piece of ceramic art—her school friends had filled it up with scribbles and drawings. She looked up and smiled at Sister Sarah. On the single bed next to hers, Geetu was in deep sleep, arms around Bhalu, her frayed brown teddy bear. With her long-lashed eyes shut and her facial muscles relaxed, she looked even younger than her fourteen years. Her shaved head rested on the pillow, right next to Bhalu, her nose buried in his ear.

She had wept loudly the day the barber was supposed to visit. But once he arrived and started snipping off her softly curling shoulder-length hair, she sat quietly, with an apron draped around her, though the tears continued to slip off her cheeks. Her surgery was repeatedly being postponed, since her haemoglobin level was low. Sarah often found herself feeling sorry for the child and for her mother, who would be with Geetu every day during visiting hours, bringing her her favourite snacks, picture books and listening to her crying when she was upset.

Sometimes, Sarah would catch Geetu looking thoughtfully at herself in the small hand mirror she kept in her drawer, when she thought no one was watching. She would hold it up with one hand and stare at her reflection while using the other hand to slowly stroke the top of her shaved head, where prickly hair had started to sprout. With her high cheek bones and bald head she looked even more beautiful now to Sarah—fragile and delicate. And she made sure she told Geetu this at least once every day. But Geetu would just blush and turn her head away or start waving her hands before her face to flick away the flies and mosquitoes that she imagined around herself whenever she was disturbed. Often, her piteous cry 'Mujhe makkhi machhar kaat rahe hain' would ring out, and Sarah would watch Geetu's gentle, soft-spoken mother pretending to shoo them away using a hand towel.

Sometimes Geetu would see imaginary people and ask for them to be told to leave. Though initially it had been eerie for those around her to find her speaking to invisible people or screaming that she wanted them to leave, they had all got used to it by now and would play along till she quieted down. Sarah hoped that the surgery to remove the tiny tumour in Geetu's head—which had started interfering with her behaviour, making her imagine things—would go off well and that she would return to a normal childhood soon.

Sarah was satisfied to note that nearly all her patients were in peaceful sleep, other than night birds like Dakshina and Colonel Aditya Rana, who had his bedside lamp on and was propped up on his pillows in his blue hospital gown, with a saline drip going into one wrist. He was engrossed in reading. Sarah stepped in to find that his drip bottle was almost empty and removed the needle deftly from his wrist, holding the punctured skin down for a minute with a swab of cotton dipped in antiseptic.

'Another James Hadley Chase, sir?' she asked, coiling up the tubes and dropping the empty saline bottle into the dustbin by his bedside. Flicking his wrist a few times to get the blood flowing, he smiled and nodded and got back to his reading with a polite, 'Goodnight, sister.'

As Sarah walked back to the duty room, a soothing peace seemed to descend over the Lansdowne Military Hospital building. The four attendants on night duty were watching TV in the recreation room. There had been an emergency at Duty Medical Officer Colonel Ranjith Rao's house, and he had rushed home, telling her to call him if he was needed. Sister Jaya had developed a severe stomach ache and had retired to the nursing hostel next to the hospital. Sarah had never been alone in the hospital before and had been a little apprehensive initially, but with no serious patients in the wards, she was beginning to enjoy the solitude.

It was an exceptionally dark night, making the stars sparkle even brighter. Tempted to get a glimpse of the night sky, Sarah walked across to where the red tin roof ended. Looking up, she stood still for a moment, soaking in the splendour of the countless stars twinkling above her head and then turned, with a sigh, to go back in. The yellow light from the bulbs hanging above her head turned her white uniform beige as she walked down the corridor, her skirt swishing softly against her legs, her hard-heeled black shoes clicking against the floor. Pulling open the creaky wooden door to the duty room, Sarah placed her tray of medicines and injections on the table, unpinned her white head scarf and poured herself a cup of strong black coffee from her flask. Breathing in its deep, intoxicating aroma, she kicked off her shoes and sat back with her head resting against the chair. She had just taken her first sip and shut her eyes to savour the coffee's comforting warmth on her tongue when there was a knock on the door. Startled, she looked up to find the hazy figure of a soldier in uniform outside the glass widow. 'Who's there?' she called out.

A handsome Sikh soldier, at least six feet tall and broad-shouldered, with a green turban covering his head, hesitantly peered in. 'May I come in, madam sahab?' he asked, his voice deep though sounding unsure.

When she nodded, he walked in. She was surprised to find his combat dress ripped in places with bloodstains over it. There was grime on his face, and his turban was frayed and coming loose at the ends. 'What happened?' she asked in alarm, reading his embroidered nametag that said 'Kartar Singh A+'.

'There was an accident,' he said, sounding slightly slurred, which made Sarah suspect he had been drinking.

Asking him to sit down on the examining stool, she took a quick look at his injuries. Apart from a few cuts and bruises that were not very deep, he seemed largely unharmed. She applied antiseptic on his injuries and asked him if he had taken a tetanus shot recently. When he replied in the negative, she took out an ampoule and a syringe and—brushing aside his 'Sahab, I am scared of injections' with a curt 'Keep your arm steady'—gave him an anti-tetanus shot. Making an entry in her duty register, she asked him for the time. He looked at his watch and said, '11.50 p.m., madam sahab.'

Sarah looked up at the duty room clock to cross-check. It was exactly midnight. 'Your watch is ten minutes slow,' she told him.

'I have a terrible headache, sahab . . .' Kartar had only started telling her when an emergency bell from one of the

wards started buzzing. It was from Room 12, Bed 1. Sarah
stood up in alarm. Dakshina's broken leg had recently been
plastered and she was being reckless about walking with
the support of the plaster. She had fallen off her wheelchair
only last week, luckily with no damage. Worried that she
might have fallen again while making a trip to the toilet,
Sarah got up.

'Sahab, my head is hurting very badly,' Kartar said.

He was definitely slurring his words, she thought, and
asked him sharply, 'Are you drunk? Pee ke aaye ho?'

'No, madam,' Kartar replied, 'I don't drink.'

Other than a faint blue bruise on his forehead, he looked
fine to her. 'Please wait. I'll come back and see you,' she said,
slipping on her shoes. While rushing out of the room, she
saw him slowly getting up from the chair, holding his head
as if in terrible pain. She thought she saw blood on his hand but
shrugged it off since he really didn't have any major injuries.
Leaving the room, she walked briskly down the corridor.

When Sarah opened the door to Room 12 she was
relieved to find Dakshina sitting on her bed, her leg intact.
Dakshina was looking at Geetu, who sat propped up on her
pillows, holding on tightly to her teddy bear. The moment
Geetu saw Sarah, she started crying. 'He has come to the
hospital. Why?' she wailed. 'Usko jaane ke liye bolo.' Sarah
could see no one, as always, but she was used to handling
the hallucinating child. Stepping forward, she shook her
hand in front of Geetu. 'Go away,' Sarah said, her voice
stern. 'Go away right now.'

Geetu was staring at her. 'He is standing behind you,' she whispered.

Sarah turned around. There was no one there but she kept up her act. 'Didn't I tell you to go?' she said, raising her voice. 'You are upsetting Geetu. Just leave. We don't want you here.'

Geetu seemed at ease. 'Wo jaa raha hai,' she said, relieved, as her eyes followed the imaginary figure out of the room.

Sarah walked across to Geetu's bedside, pulled the sheet higher up her frail body and sat next to her, gently holding her hand. Geetu slipped lower over the pillows, with her head buried in Bhalu's, and was asleep within minutes. Sarah switched off the bedside lamp and whispered 'Goodnight, darling' to Dakshina, who looked up from her diary and rolled her eyes in exasperation.

'If she wakes up again, just buzz me,' Sarah said.

'Sure.' Dakshina nodded and went back to her writing.

Sarah trudged back to the duty room. She had not shut the door in her hurry to leave and noticed that it was still open. The injured soldier, though, was nowhere to be seen. She thought he might have gone looking for a toilet, but when nearly fifteen minutes had passed and he did not return, she called up the sentry at the hospital's main gate, asking if the Sikh soldier had gone back.

The guard was confused. 'Ma'am, no one has come in after we locked the main gate for the night,' he told her.

A puzzled Sarah threw away the injection syringe and the swabs of cotton she had used for dressing the soldier's wounds. Feeling completely exhausted, she took off her shoes and lay back on the bunk bed, shutting her eyes. The moment her head hit the pillow, she drifted off to sleep.

* * *

She got up with a start to the shrill ringing of the phone and reached out for the handset. It was the Commandant. 'There is bad news, Sarah,' he said, his voice grave. 'A Shaktiman bringing twenty soldiers from Kotdwar to Lansdowne fell into a deep gorge an hour back.'

She was instantly wide awake. 'I'll get the beds prepared right away, sir,' she assured him.

'That will not be required, Sarah,' he said. 'There were no survivors.'

It was still dark but the soft orange glow of dawn had begun to spread in the sky by the time the bodies started coming in. In the mortuary, Sarah stood next to Dr Rao, who had rushed to the hospital soon after the news of the accident had come in, making entries in the documents that would be sent from the hospital to confirm the deaths.

She recognized the Sikh soldier the moment he was brought in on a stretcher. His body was being carried by two young recruits with sombre faces. She bent down to read his nameplate: 'Kartar Singh A+'. The deep purple bruise on his forehead was slowly turning black.

'He was the driver. Such a handsome boy. Probably hit his head against the steering wheel when the truck fell. Death by concussion,' Dr Rao whispered, shaking his head sadly.

Sarah's brain was flashing information in front of her eyes from the notes she had made in nursing college many years back. 'Concussion: Injury to the brain caused by impact. Common in car accidents when the neck jerks and the head is hit either in or opposite to the direction of impact. Symptoms include mild to severe headache, disorientation and slurring of speech.' She could feel her skin breaking out in goose pimples.

Dr Rao lifted Kartar Singh's limp hand and was looking at his smashed wristwatch. An old HMT. It had a crack across the dial and its hands pointed out 11.50 p.m. 'That fixes the time of the accident,' he said. 'Please make an entry, Sarah.'

Sarah's mind flashed her memories from a few hours back. A handsome face with a darkening bruise mark. A hesitant voice saying, 'May I come in, madam sahab?' Slurred speech. Her annoyance. 'Are you drunk?' 'I don't drink, madam sahab.' The duty room clock showing the time as 12 p.m. Her abrupt observation, 'Your watch is ten minutes slow.'

She bent her head and started writing in the register with trembling fingers. Kartar Singh's body lay in front of her, still and lifeless now. Rigor mortis was beginning to set in.

Face Off

The bullet had gone through him, but Lieutenant Samay Yadav was still breathing. Captain Sunil Kaul had the palm of his hand pressed firmly on the gaping, coin-sized hole in Samay's chest, but blood continued to ooze through the gaps between his fingers, staining them a dark red. It was trickling down his wrist and seeping into the edge of his olive-green shirtsleeve. The clammy feel of the fabric was making his skin crawl. He felt a desperate urge to roll up his sleeve. But he knew that if he lifted his hand, even for a second, a gushing fountain of blood would spurt from Samay's wound, causing his blood pressure to fall further.

'Ishwar, meri kameez ki bazu upar kar de,' he told the soldier kneeling by his side, who had a rifle on his shoulder, a helmet on his head, a bulletproof vest covering his chest and a face strained with worry. Kaul's eyes moved back to the young officer lying on his back, lifeless, his heaving chest the only sign that he was alive. He had led a platoon of men to surround the house where, according to the intel they had received, a suspected militant was hiding. The villagers had completely denied the presence of any militant, with the Gaon Budha, the lanky old village head with matted hair, a wrinkled face and intelligent eyes, shaking his head grimly. 'Aapka information galat hai, leftinant sahab. Fauj hamein pareshan kar rahi hai,' he had said.

Samay—gentle, soft-spoken, courteous as always—had been polite but firm. He had insisted that his boys would not leave without conducting a house-to-house search. He would lead it personally, he'd said, ensuring that no one was unnecessarily troubled. 'I trust you, baba. But please understand that we have received information, and I cannot go back without checking it. If we find no one, we will leave.'

The dogs barked. The children stopped their games. The women chattered in displeasure. The men scowled. But Samay had ignored them all. 'Follow me,' he had told his men—soldiers with expressionless faces and rifles on their shoulders—who had been waiting patiently for orders. They had immediately lined up behind the young Company Commander, a man they loved and respected.

It turned out the intelligence report was correct. Just that they had got the numbers wrong. There were more than five militants hiding in the old two-storey house, right next to the village head's. Not only were they fully armed, they were also completely aware of the army's movement. They had watched the soldiers from an upstairs window, waited for them to come close and then opened fire, shooting the leading section of three at point-blank range. Since Samay had been right in front, he had been the first to take a bullet, unfortunately straight in the chest. The two soldiers behind him were the next to fall.

Though the rest of the company, led by the fearless Subedar Yudhvir Singh, Shaurya Chakra, quickly closed in and a nasty gunfight had ensued, the soldiers had their hands tied, due to the presence of women on the ground floor who were cooking for the militants. Yudhvir and his men stormed the house, strictly following Samay's orders that no civilians should be hurt. This had restricted their movements, and the militants had managed to jump out of a window at the back of the house, disappearing into the shadows of dusk.

Yudhvir Singh ordered an immediate cordon around the small cluster of less than ten houses, but he knew that the chances of finding the militants were near zero. They knew the area like the back of their hands and would have slunk deep into the jungles of Jairampur. A shattered Yudhvir left the rest of the soldiers in cordon, while he and Ishwar lifted Samay, who was the only one of the three casualties still breathing. They crossed the shallow stream, ran across the jungle and, panting in exertion, managed to carry Samay back to where their unit doctor, Captain Sunil Kaul, was waiting. A radio message had already been sent, asking the battalion to immediately provide an ambulance. The bodies of the two dead soldiers were brought back subsequently.

Yudhvir had been a young soldier when Lt Col Yadav, Samay's father, had come to the unit with his young wife and school-going son. He had seen Samay grow from a wide-eyed little boy into a handsome, young, newly commissioned officer. The day he saw Samay in uniform for the first time, Yudhvir had saluted him with a wide smile on his face. Samay had stepped forward to embrace him warmly saying, 'Kaise ho, Yudhvir Bhaiya?' and continued addressing him as 'Bhaiya' even after he had taken over as the Company Commander of Alfa Company, though Yudhvir had started addressing him as sahab instead of Samu, as they all used to call him in childhood . . .

Memories flooded his brain as he watched Kaul fix the drip.

* * *

Ishwar Chand removed his rifle from his shoulder, placed it on the grass and bent forward to unbutton Kaul's shirtsleeve. The thick fabric was soaked in blood and his fingers struggled with the tight buttonhole but he managed to roll it up. Taking off his own helmet, he placed it on the grass beside his rifle and went back to sitting on his haunches, his shirt front stiff from Samay's blood. It was now drying in the breeze and caking into a dull red crust.

The bullet was lodged somewhere inside Samay's chest, but Kaul made no effort to locate it. He had learnt in medical school that extricating an object from an open chest wound might cause more harm than leaving it there. He concentrated instead on keeping the wound closed. It was a little below the left nipple, and with the flat of his palm covering it, Kaul could feel Samay's ribs move under his fingers each time he tried to breathe. He could see pain, mingled with the desperation to survive, on Samay's sweat-soaked face. 'Himmat rakh, Samay. Nothing will happen to you,' he said.

Samay opened his mouth to say something. His lips moved but he was unable to form the words. 'The ambulance is on its way. Just keep breathing, buddy.' Kaul looked tenderly at the dark and handsome face, its features twisted in pain and extreme exhaustion, simply from the task of breathing. Kaul's eyes moved to the needle lodged in Samay's arm, slowly dripping saline into him. And then, his gaze involuntarily shifted to what he had consciously avoided looking at: the other two casualties, laid out under the shade of the same tree. Barely twenty years of age. And both gone. His eyes clouded over with sadness. He couldn't do anything for them. They were brought to him dead.

* * *

'How long is the ambulance going to take, Yudhvir Sahab?' He turned his head to look at the tall and hefty Junior Commissioned Officer standing next to his radio operator—a young boy not older than nineteen—whose name Kaul did not know. He heard the radio set crackle.

'Raasta bahut kharab hai, sa'ab. They are driving through the jungle,' Yudhvir told him. 'They will take at least twenty minutes to reach the main road. And then ten more minutes to climb up to us.'

Kaul was well aware that gunshot wounds to the chest were considered the most dangerous kind of emergency. He had initially tried to stuff a thick wad of cotton into the opening, but the plug kept getting pushed out by the continuous bleeding. So now he was trying his best to close the wound with his hand. Blood loss was not his only worry. He realized that more danger was posed by the air that might be getting sucked into Samay's chest. It could lead to a lung collapse. Though his muscles were starting to ache, Kaul increased the pressure and made sure his palm closed the hole as tightly as he could.

This was the second gunshot injury he was handling in a month, and Kaul's heart filled with sorrow each time he thought about the first. His own nursing assistant, Rifleman Randhir, shot in the neck while dragging an injured soldier behind a rock, just a week back. He wasn't even carrying a rifle at that time. In his hands, there was a morphine injection that he wanted to administer to the soldier crying in pain at having his knee shattered by a burst of bullets. On his shoulder, there was a backpack filled with medicines and field dressing. Not yet thirty and sent back home in a body bag. And the ignominy of a death that did not come while he was defending his country against an external enemy but was simply the result of him getting in the way of a bullet. Killed in a battle against his own people. Combatting insurgency was not the army's job; this was not what Rifleman Randhir had joined the army for. And certainly not what Kaul had joined for either.

After the initial shock of Randhir's death had settled, Kaul had asked for an interview with his Commanding Officer. Saluting him, Kaul had said he wanted to leave the army. One of his college classmates was running an NGO in a village in Maharashtra to provide basic healthcare in backward areas, and Kaul felt he would be able to serve his country better there.

His CO had given him a patient hearing, called him home for dinner and told him with great affection to go home on a month's leave and rethink his decision. 'Your application is in my drawer and I shall process it after you come back. The army has to fight this ugly war. Collateral damage cannot be avoided. Innocent people sometimes die in wars and we have to accept that. Think it over, and we shall have another conversation after you come back. With a status update, right?' the CO asked with a smile. He knew that Kaul was getting married soon.

Kaul's leave was to begin fifteen days later.

* * *

Samay's eyes had fluttered open. He moaned softly, his breath coming out in painful gasps. The grim-faced Yudhvir was wiping the beads of sweat collecting on the young lieutenant's forehead. 'Sa'ab, kuch nahi hoga aapko. Hausla rakho,' he was saying.

As the unit doctor, Kaul was supposed to inspire confidence in others. He was supposed to stay in control of the situation. He had been telling himself this repeatedly, each time panic rose in his heart, but he was just a rookie captain of the Army Medical Corps. 'Don't take any chances. Treat any wound caused by chest penetration as a sucking chest wound.' He remembered his Department of Surgery professor saying this at Pune's Armed Forces Medical College during a lecture on emergency medicine. 'When a person's chest is punctured, each time the injured expands his chest cavity to inhale, air not only goes in through the mouth and nose, it also goes in through the hole which can lead to a collapse of the lungs,' the professor had explained to the class. Kaul hoped as hell that this was not happening in Samay's body.

* * *

Ten more minutes had passed. The three soldiers still sat silently around Samay. He had not properly opened his eyes once. Amid the rustle of the wind blowing dry leaves around them, they could hear soft, hissing sounds each time Samay tried to breathe in or out. Kaul prayed desperately that the ambulance would get to them in time. Looking up, he found Yudhvir tilting the cap of his water bottle slowly, to let water trickle into Samay's open mouth.

'Don't give him water, sahab,' Kaul snapped. A startled Yudhvir pulled his arm back. Kaul's own hand had moved slightly and his fingers were suddenly soaked in warm blood. He quickly repositioned his palm.

'Paani,' Samay's frail voice was pleading.

'Take some wet cotton and moisten his lips. We'll give him water only after we reach the hospital,' Kaul told Yudhvir.

Yudhvir did as he was told. 'I used to be senior Colonel Yadav sa'ab's sahayak. Samay sa'ab ke father,' he told Kaul. 'I used to take him to school on my bicycle. Once, his foot was caught in the steel rim of the moving wheel and was cut badly,' he said softly, speaking to himself more than anyone else. 'I took him straight to the MI room. He buried his head in my chest when they were stitching the wound. Bola, "Bhaiya, please Mummy ko mat batana."'

Samay opened his eyes. He was looking at them anxiously. 'You'll be fine,' Kaul told him, ensuring that his voice did not convey any worry. A strange, bubbling sound had started issuing from deep inside Samay's throat. His lips were turning blue. The veins on his neck had suddenly distended, appearing taut on his slim neck. Yudhvir was helplessly holding on to Samay's spasming body. His chest had sunk in on one side. The other side seemed to be enlarging. Kaul knew that a lung had collapsed. Samay's breath was becoming slow and laborious. Asking Ishwar to cover the chest wound, Kaul bent forward. Pinching Samay's nose shut, he started giving him mouth-to-mouth resuscitation. But there was no response. He looked up to find that Samay's breath had stopped. His eyes were open but glassy.

Kaul sat down on the grass. His arms hanging limply by his sides. Tears of grief and frustration in his eyes. Ishwar looked at Kaul and pulled his hand away, rocking back and forth on his haunches, watching the blood seeping out of his dead Company Commander's chest. Then, he began to sob loudly. Yudhvir looked up in disbelief. 'Why did you give up, Doctor Sa'ab?' he asked, staring at Samay's lifeless body.

Wiping his blood-stained hand on his shirt, Kaul closed Samay's eyes gently. 'Ab kuch nahi ho sakta, Yudhvir Sahab,' he said.

Yudhvir was aghast. 'He would have commanded our unit one day. He had laughed loudly when I had told him that and said, "You would retire by then, Yudhvir Bhaiya. But promise me you will come for my darbar in a black bandgala suit."'

Yudhvir's voice was hoarse. He was talking to himself. 'Yadav Sa'ab ne bola tha mujhe, "Samay ka dhyan rakhna, Yudhvir. Bachcha hai abhi, koi experience nahi hai. Don't let him take any unnecessary risks." How will I face him again?' he mumbled. And then his voice seemed to change. 'Mujhe hi kuch karna padega.'

* * *

Kaul raised his eyes to look at Yudhvir. He was surprised to find grief replaced by an eerie calm.

Yudhvir was strapping on his bulletproof vest. 'Ishwar, khada ho. It's time for action,' he said, jamming his helmet on his head and pushing the chin strap into its buckle. 'Aur tu sun meri baat,' he snapped at the radio set operator. 'Tell the platoon to start moving the cordon forward slowly. Saari nafri. I shall be there in ten minutes,' he said, his voice cold and seething in fury.

A cold shiver ran down Kaul's spine. 'Kya kar rahe hain, Yudhvir Sahab?' he asked.

'Badla le rahe hain, sahab,' Yudhvir replied, reaching out for his rifle. 'We will burn the village.'

Kaul looked at him in disbelief. 'The militants would have run away by now. Only the villagers remain. Kis se badla lenge?'

Yudhvir's face was an expressionless mask. He was staring far into the distance. 'They lied to us. We will teach them a lesson they will never forget.'

Kaul was horrified. 'There are women and children in the village. You are a decorated soldier. You can't do this.' Standing up, he placed a hand on Yudhvir's arm. 'Call the platoon back. We will return to camp and take revenge on the militant group when the time comes,' he said, trying to reason with Yudhvir, as one would with a child.

'Sorry, sa'ab. This shall be done today,' Yudhvir said curtly. 'You don't need to worry. You are not party to it. You stay here with the bodies.'

* * *

Dusk had fallen, and when he turned his head in the
direction of the village where the gunfight had happened,
Kaul could see the flicker of lanterns. A few chimneys were
smoking. The hens must be back in their coops, the pigs
in their sties under the bamboo huts; the rosy-cheeked
children with runny noses were probably inside their
homes, awaiting dinner.

'Your Company Commander is dead, Yudhvir
Sahab,' Kaul said, his voice firm. 'I might be a doctor
but I am also an officer of the unit. I am taking over the
company. Aap mera aadesh manenge.' He turned to face
the trembling radio operator. 'Call the soldiers back. This
is an order.'

Yudhvir met his gaze unflinchingly. 'You are an
outsider, sa'ab. How long have you been with the men?
Two years. I have been with them for thirty. They will not
listen to you.'

Kaul's hands were shaking. 'Stop, Yudhvir Sahab! Or I
shall report you. You are retiring from service in ten days.
You don't want to end up in jail.' He stepped in front of
Yudhvir.

Yudhvir snapped his rifle open to slip in a cartridge.
Pointing the gun at Kaul, he said, 'Aap mujhe majboor kar
rahe hain, sa'ab . . .'

* * *

Author's note: At this point in the story, the reader is offered two different endings. You may choose to read one or both, and then decide whichever works for you.

* * *

Alpha

Kaul was shocked. 'Ab aap mujhe maroge, sahab? Will killing me or burning the village bring Samay Sahab back?' Stepping forward, he slapped Yudhvir's face.

Yudhvir looked at him with tormented eyes and pulled back the safety catch on his rifle. An ominous click rang out. It was followed by a shot and a scream. Birds that had been settling for the night called out in surprise; the wind whistled through the blades of grass; there was a squeal of tyres.

'Ambulance pahunch gayi hai, sa'ab,' Ishwar called out.

'Run down. Double speed. Get the stretchers,' said Yudhvir, rifle in hand, staring down at the doctor's lifeless body lying at his feet. He then looked up to meet Ishwar's scared eyes. 'All four were killed in the encounter. Samajh gaya?' Ishwar nodded and lowered his eyes.

Yudhvir turned around to look at the frightened radio operator. 'Tell the platoon, I shall be with them in ten minutes,' he said. 'And then put on your bulletproof vest and come along.'

With that, Yudhvir bent down to pick up the empty cartridge lying near the doctor's lifeless body and headed into the dense bamboo thicket, tears flowing down his cheeks.

* * *

Bravo

Kaul was shocked. 'Ab aap mujhe maroge, sahab? Killing me or setting the village on fire will not get your Samay Sahab back. I will not let you do this,' he said, looking into Yudhvir's tormented eyes.

Yudhvir pulled the safety catch on his rifle. The birds were chirping noisily in their nests. The wind whistled through the blades of grass. There was a squeal of tyres on the road below.

'Ambulance pahunch gayi hai, sa'ab,' Ishwar called out.

Kaul took a quick step towards Yudhvir, slapped him hard on the face and took the rifle from his hands. 'Bodies load karwao,' he said.

Fifteen days later

An army bus is slowly winding its way through the lush green forests of Arunachal, where orchids dip down from trees and a blue-green river gurgles alongside the road, its white, sandy bank sparkling in the sunlight. It is part of the convoy taking soldiers to the Guwahati Transit Camp, from where they will board trains and flights to their hometowns.

There is an air of bonhomie inside, since the soldiers are looking forward to meeting their families and loved ones. Yudhvir is staring out of the window, the wind ruffling his hair. 'Kya soch rahe hain, Yudhvir Sahab,' asks the good-looking young officer sitting next to him in jeans and a collared white T-shirt.

Yudhvir turns to look at him and says, 'Sahab, I was wondering why you did not report my behaviour that day.'

Kaul smiles. 'This vardi that we both decided to wear makes us brothers in life, in death, in happiness, in sadness and in moments of extreme emotional turmoil,' he says. 'If a soldier cannot understand another soldier's pain, who will?'

'I have to admit, Doctor Sa'ab,' Yudhvir says. 'You are a brave man. You weren't scared. Not even for a moment.'

'Shall I tell you the truth, Yudhvir Sahab?' Kaul answers in all seriousness. 'You had scared me to death. Par main acting achchi kar leta hun.'

Both break into loud laughter that has the other soldiers shaking their heads and smiling. Kaul slips a hand into his sling bag and passes an envelope to Yudhvir.

'I am getting married, sahab,' he says. 'You will have to be there. In a black bandgale ka suit.'

'Zarur aaunga, sa'ab. Suit silwana padega,' Yudhvir replies, leaning his head back on the seat and closing his eyes. He can see Samay smiling from somewhere far away.

A Macabre Tale

With his crisp, upturned moustache, grey beard and wine-red turban, the Colonel cut a stylish figure, even at fifty. When he tucked his stomach in and walked with that purposeful gait twenty-nine years of wearing the olive-green uniform had given him, he commanded attention—even if he was only making his way to the stiff Patiala peg of whisky that awaited him at the bar.

'Sahib' was what his new wife (the second Mrs Shergill), younger to him by seventeen years, called him, never being audacious enough to address him by his first name. And that's why the neighbours said she would last. 'She is a smart one, this Reenu, not like the other one who was stupid enough to show the maid the scar behind her ear, where the back of her earring had made a gash from having her head slammed against the wall,' they whispered.

The Colonel enjoyed parties and the company of women. Clinking ice cubes in his glass, he always gravitated to where the ladies were, greeting them with an exaggerated bow of his handsome head. His flashing eyes would find his wife, more than a decade younger than the plump, ageing partners of his envious course mates, and a wave of pride in this new possession would overwhelm him. She was eager to please, and he already had her saying 'Good evening' in the polished tones of a convent-educated girl, something he could never teach his first wife.

He would sometimes recall the horror of his earlier marriage—twenty-nine years spent with a fat, dark, illiterate village woman, who wore a long plait, a big, maroon, stick-on bindi and had spare tyres of fat piling around the waist. It was a match fixed by his father, the late Sardar Himmat Singh Shergill, none of whose five sons ever dared say no to him. The old Sardar Sahab, a man of his word, had gone to visit a dying friend in the village and promised him that he would take care of his motherless daughter. He had brought her home in the train, bought her five new pairs of salwar kameez, two gold bangles, a grand phulkari dupatta and ordered his newly commissioned son to take pheras with her in the gurudwara and keep her happy for life. A young captain at that time, a Commando Dagger from Infantry School with a bright future ahead of him, he could not say no, even though he found her uncouth and ordinary.

She had turned out to be a devoted wife—keeping house, bearing him three children, looking after his parents, cooking butter chicken for the family every weekend and rajma chawal twice in the week, even desperately powdering her dark cheeks in a futile attempt to look fair. The years went by, their kids grew up. They had a working relationship but no companionship. While she remained his devoted partner, he could never bring himself to love her, immersing himself completely in work, opting for field postings whenever it was possible. When he was home on leave, she fawned over him, oiling his waist-length hair every Sunday, knotting them on top of his head and massaging his feet. Sometimes, she would pluck white hair from his moustache, taking pleasure in his good looks, while he disdained her ordinariness.

And then one evening, as he sat alone in the veranda of the old, secluded British-era bungalow they lived in, listening to Jagjit Singh's ghazals with a glass of whisky in his hands, watching the rain fall, he decided that he wanted to be free of her. It had been four years since his father died. The children had gone away—their elder daughter had got married to an NRI from Canada; their son had joined the army; and their youngest daughter, an exceptionally bright student since childhood, had gone away to medical college.

That Sunday there was a thunderstorm, and flashes of lightning shot across the monsoon sky. She had washed her hair, their ends dripping water over the tiles, and was standing barefoot before the Granth Sahib, where she did her paath every morning. Bending slightly to light the jyot, one hand cupped around the match to stop the flame from dying out, she didn't turn around when he came from behind, treading lightly, just as he had been trained to do many years back, during his commando course. The pistol

had been an inch from her forehead. The silencer attached.
His hand had been steady, as always. In a flash, it was over.

The jyot was still burning when the ambulance came,
and those who had gathered around, having heard the gun
shot, admired the strength in his biceps and the dignity
on his face when he stepped out carrying his dead wife
in his arms. She was depressed after the kids left and had
committed suicide, shooting herself with the pistol he had
so affectionately taught her how to use. So it was believed,
though he never said a word about it in public. And no one
ever asked.

* * *

A year and half had passed. He stared at the gathering
where his new wife sat smiling. She had smoky, kohl-
rimmed eyes and was draped in an embroidered red silk
sari. Fragrant mogra flowers bloomed in her hair, with red
sindoor glowing in the parting. He had found her in a poor
family in the village that was proud to have a Colonel Sa'ab
as their son-in-law. He had been helping them financially
for a few years and had noticed the pretty young girl in
faded cotton salwar suits. He had been quick to notice the
star-struck look in her eyes when he would drive by in his
black Scorpio, his dark glasses flashing.

The moment he had the proposal conveyed to her
father, through the village sarpanch, her family agreed.
They thought a year was a decent span of time to wait after

the demise of his first wife, and then they had gone for a simple marriage, with the Colonel bearing all the costs. Many happy years awaited him. It was a lovely picture, marred only by the memory of a hazy face—of a dark, big-cheeked woman, with a crimson stain spreading from a hole in her forehead into her ear and on to his shirtsleeve.

'Collateral damage is accepted in wars. To win battles, lives often have to be sacrificed,' the voice of his academy instructor in Warfare and Tactics rang out in his ears. The Colonel raised his glass in the direction of his blushing wife, emptied it and moved back to the bar for a refill.

The Siachen Rescue

On the Siachen glacier—named after the pink sia blossoms that bloom across Ladakh in the summer months—another long winter had fallen. Movement between the Siachen base camp and Point 4212 had ceased and would resume only when the summer sun melted the snow next year.

No flowers bloomed in Siachen. A perpetual blanket of thick snow ensured that all life lay smothered. At this time of the year, the blanket got thicker, hiding the mouths of crevasses and obscuring the edges of precipices to the extent that it became impossible to tell where a man could step safely and where the snow would give way under his feet, sending him hurtling down to a painful death.

Point 4212 was a winter-cutoff post, which meant that it got snowed up during winter, and even helicopters could not fly there to drop rations and medical supplies. Every September, food and kerosene were stocked up at the post, emergency medicines distributed and emotional hugs exchanged between the soldiers stationed at the air-maintained base camp and those who were to man Point 4212. A team of seven would then begin its long journey across the icy terrain, walking for nearly six hours, to reach the small fibre-glass hut that was going to be their home through the rest of winter. For these soldiers, it would be the longest six months of their lives. The falling snow would completely cut them off from the rest of the world. Only when the snow melted in March, and a new lot was here to replace them, would they trek back to the base camp and eventually head home.

During these lonely months spent in subzero temperatures, the soldiers derived warmth from two sources: a kerosene bukhari that burnt inside their fibre-glass hut 24/7; and Madhuri Dixit in a yellow sari, smiling at them from a poster on the wall. The vagaries of the weather had caused the sari to fade in places, but the magic of her smile was intact and it still possessed the power to take the chill off frozen hearts.

The only visitors to Point 4212 during this lonely stretch were Pista and Pisti, two large and friendly Gaddi strays, who lived in the base camp, camping near its cookhouse most of the time, drawn by the aroma of fresh rotis being tossed on the heavy iron griddle and cauldrons of meat simmering in the langar. Over the years, they had been trained to carry letters to Point 4212 for a reward of fish and meat. Having completely adapted to the hostile weather, they were light-footed despite their size and experts at navigating surface ice that could easily crack under a man's weight.

Every week, when a friendly Cheetah helicopter dropped down parcels of letters meant for the soldiers, along with gunnysacks of food and medicine at the base camp, the mail for Peak 4212 would be carefully sifted out and tied around the dogs' necks. The two would immediately head for the post, knowing that tinned meat and a warm welcome awaited them there. After spending some time with the soldiers at 4212, they would return to the base camp, making another trip only when the next consignment of letters arrived.

* * *

Lately, a new canine companion had started accompanying Pista and Pisti on their weekly forays. He was a big dog, with a lush coat and a muddy white tail that curved like a fat cashew nut, which was why the soldiers had started calling him Kaju. While Pista and Pisti would jump on the men, lick their faces and arch their backs to rub against the soldiers' trouser legs, Kaju would not indulge in any such crass displays of affection. He was a loner who kept to himself and stepped cautiously closer to the men only when food was offered. Otherwise, he would just sit at a distance in the snow, tightly coiled up with his big black nose tucked under his tail to avoid the chill. Any attempts at familiarity were rebuffed with a deep growl. Kaju was

doing the long trek only for the meat, and he made no . . .
well . . . bones about it.

Kaju had also started making the occasional lone trip to
Point 4212. The men would sometimes find him outside
their hut, where he would be barking gruffly to make his
presence felt. Desperate for company, they would greet
him with exclamations of joy. While he would stolidly
ignore the soldiers, Kaju would devour food offerings in
large, greedy mouthfuls and lick his white enamel plate
clean. He would then shake the snow off his matted fur
and make his way back to the base camp. So far, he hadn't
brought any letters, but his visits were still welcome. For
the lonely men ticking the days off in their minds, he was a
sign that life awaited them across the frozen glacier.

One morning, the men were shaken out of their ennui
by their young Company Commander, Captain Ranvijay
Singh, a handsome sardar, though now sporting a beard
that looked like an overgrown forest. 'Khade ho jao mere
sheron. Let's complete our patrol before the weather packs
up,' he declared, thumping the slim and slightly-built
Rifleman Ranjit Rajwada hard on his back. With that,
Ranvijay moved out of the fibre-glass hut, adjusting his
snow goggles over his eyes.

Rajwada quickly put on his snow boots, reached for his
own goggles and stepped out after him, surveying the sea
of white all around and the sky that appeared to be slowly
turning grey. He marvelled at the world of sharp contrasts
that the glacier was. Just this morning, the sun had been

so intense and fierce that he had gone out of the hut in his combat T-shirt and returned with sunburnt arms. Soon after, clouds had started gathering and the temperature dipped to below freezing point.

Everyone on the glacier knew that clear skies were invariably followed by blizzards and snow storms, when the wind screamed at 150 kmph, capable of dismantling communication antennae, overturning unanchored snowmobiles and ripping off the door of their fibre-glass hut. And before every impending storm the soldiers had to perform a compulsory drill. A patrol would go out to check if the communication wires—their lifeline—were in order.

* * *

'We should be back in two hours. Maximum three. Otherwise we'll get caught in the storm. Let's not waste any time,' Ranvijay told his patrol of Rajwada and the other four who had joined them by then. The soldiers, all clad in their snowsuits, faces covered with thick olive-green balaclavas and large goggles, nodded agreement. Tied to each other by ropes—so that if a man fell into a crevice the others could pull him out—the soldiers left the hut and started following the communication lines. Their job was to check if the wires were getting buried in snow at any point, pull those out and prop them up against snow-filled jerry cans. Progress was painfully slow. The temperature had dipped below minus 40 degrees Celsius, and even though they had become used to it now, walking at 21,000 feet strained their lungs, with the oxygen-deficient air making breathing extremely difficult. The weight of their triple-layered snowsuits and boots made every step an achievement, and covering a distance of twenty metres often took them an hour because of the sheer effort involved. As the men slowly made their way through the bleak landscape, they could see the huts of the Pakistanis far in the distance—grey specks in endless white, giving a sense of purpose to their lonely foray.

Making sure everything was in place and reaching the end of their marked area, Ranvijay gave a shake to the rope with a flick of his sturdy wrist. It was a set signal to the patrol to turn and head back for their shelter. The men at the other end of the rope had already turned around when they thought they heard soft whimpering sounds. These seemed to be coming from inside a crevasse that the soldiers had just crossed. Since he was closest to it, Rajwada walked up to the edge of the bottomless gaping hole and peered in. He could make out the fuzzy outline of a big dog, stuck some twenty metres below on a narrow jutting in the mountainside. As his eyes adjusted to the shadows, he recognized Kaju. The dog, too, had sensed his presence and was barking piteously now, taking care that the force of his barking did not throw him off the ledge he had balanced himself on. Rajwada guessed that Kaju had probably been on his way to Point 4212 when he had fallen into the crevasse and that he had been lucky enough to land on a jutting rock, which had broken his descent. Kaju was unharmed for now, but there was no way he could come out on his own.

* * *

Turning to face his comrades, Rajwada apprised them, in his typical, no-nonsense style, of the situation. 'It's Kaju,' he said. 'He has fallen into the crevasse. He will die if we don't rescue him.'

'We have to save his life, sahabji,' declared Rifleman Hoshiyar Singh, peering in cautiously from behind Rajwada. A tall and hefty Jat, who had a wife, four children and two dogs in his village in Haryana, Hoshiyar was publicly exhibiting signs of human feelings for the first time.

'Are you crazy?' Ranvijay cut him short. 'I can't afford to lose a man trying to save a dog.'

A passionate discussion followed. The majority opinion was that Kaju couldn't be left behind; that if they were to do so, he would die. But Ranvijay was apprehensive about the risk involved. Besides, it was getting late. They were anticipating a storm, and their camp was more than an hour's trek away.

But Hoshiyar Singh was adamant. 'Buddy hai hamara, sa'ab. We can't leave him to die,' he stated sullenly, volunteering to go down the crevasse himself.

'I'm also feeling bad for him, but we can't take this risk.' Ranvijay was getting exasperated. 'You are a married man. If anything happens to you, I am answerable not just to your family but also to the Commanding Officer. What will I tell them? Kutta bachane gaya tha, mar gaya?'

Rajwada, who wasn't particularly fond of dogs and had been listening to the altercation silently so far, finally asked Ranvijay to allow him to go down the abyss. He had recently returned topping the mountaineering course at the High Altitude Warfare School, and he believed that the ice would take his weight better as he was leaner than the others. 'I'm not married either, sa'ab. You won't have answer to my wife,' he joked.

Finally, it was decided that Rajwada would go on the dog rescue mission. A rope was tied around his waist, and he was slowly lowered down the vertical face of the mountain. At the opposite end, two soldiers held on to the rope, a part of which was wrapped around the waist of the hefty Hoshiyar Singh. With an ice pick in one gloved hand and the thick nylon rope in the other, Rajwada slowly started climbing down. The sheer drop made it difficult for him to find a footing, and at every lunge he had to kick with his spiked boot to get a foothold in the wall of snow, thus descending one step at a time. After a tricky thirty minutes, Rajwada finally reached the ledge from where Kaju, his tail uncharacteristically tucked between his legs, was watching him. Digging his spiked boots into the ice, Rajwada reached out to grab the dog, so that he could hold him in his arms and ask to be pulled out. But the next moment, those waiting up on the edge of the crevasse were startled to hear a sharp cry of pain.

An alarmed Ranvijay looked down into the darkness and hollered, asking Rajwada what had happened.

'He bit me, sa'ab,' Rajwada yelled back, mouthing the choicest expletives. 'My thick gloves saved me.'

A scared and confused Kaju, who was not comfortable with humans, continued to bare his teeth and snarl menacingly even as Rajwada glared at him. He was starting to realize that it was not possible to rescue the big dog against its will.

'Forget him. Just get out. The weather is packing up,' Ranvijay's muffled voice reached him.

Rajwada could feel the sweat freezing on his palms and sharp needles of ice pricking into his hands. Though he didn't really have any love lost for Kaju, Rajwada was not one to give up easily.

He tried to make some soothing noises to comfort the dog and made one more attempt to get close to him, but the frightened Kaju continued to snarl back. 'Tujhe toh main lekar hi jaunga, saale kutte,' Rajwada, hanging in midair, his weight supported by the ice pick in his right hand, growled at him. 'Ham fauji hain. Apne saathiyon ko kabhi marne ke liye nahi chhortey.'

'Get back right now, Rajwada!' He could hear his company commander screaming from somewhere above his head.

'Ek try aur maarne do, sa'abji,' Rajwada yelled back. 'Drop me a rope, and pull when I call out.'

A fat rope quickly slithered by, and Rajwada tied its end into a loose lasso. Moving closer to the snarling dog, he flung the noose around Kaju's furry neck with one calculated move. He then tugged it tight with a yank even as Kaju bared his sharp teeth. 'Pull!' Rajwada shouted. Before the startled dog knew what was happening, the rope had pulled him off the ledge, and he was dangling from his neck above the bottomless pit.

The men at the top pulled with all their might and were surprised to find the dog hanging at its end. The knot was quickly loosened and the noose taken off. Kaju sat on his haunches, too dazed to move. Meanwhile, Rajwada was pulled up as well. He emerged panting for breath.

Ranvijay looked worried. But then Rajwada said, 'Jai Hind, sa'ab! Task pura kar diya. Bacha liya kutte ko.' He was grinning from ear to ear, his nose bright pink and eyes watering from the cold.

'Bacha liya? Behnchod, you nearly killed the bloody dog yourself. Phansi pe taang diya tha usko,' Ranvijay said, laughing in relief and stepping forward to give Rajwada a clumsy hug.

Hoshiyar Singh was watching with a gentle smile on his rugged and sunburnt face. 'Sa'abji, you went to an angreji school. But let me tell you the moral of this story,' he offered, towering over Rajwada and his Company

Commander at this emotional moment. 'Dawg ijj man's best frand.'

'Abey nahi, saale. The moral of this story is: sometimes man is dawg's best frand,' Ranvijay drawled as the men broke into raucous laughter.

They watched as Kaju made a quick recovery. The dog slowly stood up, dusted the snow off his thick fur with a brisk shake, lifted his tail in its trademark arch and set off in the direction of the base camp without so much as a look of gratitude or a wag of thank you. Rajwada watched Kaju walk away and disappear into the ocean of white. He then turned towards his waiting comrades and tied himself to the rope holding the soldiers together. They slowly made their way back to Peak 4212 in single file, with the rays of the setting sun turning their snowsuits a dull orange. On that day, summer didn't seem so far away.

* * *

Author's note: This is a fictionalized account of an actual dog rescue carried out in Siachen by soldiers of the Parachute Regiment.

The Delusion

I knew I was going to die. The blade had sliced through
my left wrist. A deep red stain was slowly spreading
across the soft cotton bedsheet. I looked at my right wrist.
A similar cloud of red was darkening the sheet there too.
My mind was fuzzy with the drug. It clouded my thinking,
dulled my responses and made me immune to the pain.
My heavy, sleepy eyes met Viju's. She was leaning back on
our son's study chair, hands loosely resting on its wooden
arms, looking straight at me. The blade was in her right
hand, grey, shiny, innocuous; its gleaming, sharp edge
covered with my blood.

'Viju,' I whispered hoarsely. 'Why?'

She kept staring at me but her eyes were blank. She
didn't seem to understand what I was saying.

Behind her, the window was open. Outside, in the
lawn, I could see Reddy, my faithful buddy from my
bachelor days in the regiment, digging up a patch of the
garden. Mastana, our handsome double-coated Alsatian,
was growling at a passer-by. Reddy had put his spade down

and was pacifying the dog. He was stroking Mastana's huge head gently while saying something in his ear. Mastana listened for a while, one ear cocked, and then started wagging his beautiful red-brown tail. Reddy picked up the spade again and returned to his gardening. If I called out to him, he would just drop everything and come running. He was very attached to me. But I had no strength left. I could barely speak.

The monsoon clouds had been drawing closer, darkening the July sky, and it looked like it would rain soon. It was the kind of weather Viju had loved till a year ago. Most monsoon evenings, she would be in the kitchen at the first sign of rain, whipping up a batter of chickpea flour, slicing onions and potatoes for the crisp yellow pakoras that she would bring out on a tray with steaming cups of tea and some green mint chutney; calling out to Reddy, asking him to take his share from the kitchen; scolding Mastana for being too close to the table, his nose twitching, knowing he was sure to get a bite too. Then, sitting down opposite me, on the white, stringed garden chairs we would drag to the veranda. Picking up a pakora, dipping it in chutney and taking a tiny bite from it, smiling at me. Rolling her big beautiful eyes to say, 'Nice, na?' Waiting for me to smile back. She had made my life so perfect in those years. Then she started changing. Right in front of my eyes. And nothing could ever be the same again.

* * *

I think it started the morning she told me she had heard voices outside our bedroom in the night. 'There are people in our house, Etta,' she said, sitting across from me at the breakfast table, almost making me choke on the filter coffee I was sipping. 'They walk around our house in the night. They listen in from behind the door. They talk to each other after we go to sleep,' she said, making me wonder for a moment if she was just pulling my leg and would break into a giggle. She wasn't. When I had brushed off her remarks with a laugh, asking her to wake me up the next time it happened, she had looked at me sadly and said, 'You don't believe me any more, Krishnetta. The trust is gone from our relationship.' She did not mention the voices ever again, much to my relief, and I too never brought up the topic, hoping she had forgotten the incident.

About a month later, I came home for lunch one afternoon to find her very upset. She told me that Mrs Chand, our neighbour, had visited. 'She came in the morning to borrow some curd, Krishnetta,' she said, pouring me a glass of hot, spicy rasam, and then her voice dropped to a shocked whisper. 'You know what? Colonel Chand beats her. She showed me the red marks on her neck. He tried to strangle her last night. He has been abusing her since they got married.'

'But they look happily married to me. They were laughing together when we came back from the party last night,' I told her, completely unsettled by her story.

She was shaking her head gravely. 'That's just an act he puts up when other people are around. She says he is a different man the moment he enters the house. He even beats up the boys. She said he once stuffed Raju's mouth with red chillies because he saw him eating greedily at the mess party. He made him stand in a corner and did not let him drink any water to teach him a lesson.'

'Why doesn't Mrs Chand go to the Army Wives Welfare Association? They take a very serious view of these kinds of things,' I told her, disregarding her demand that I speak to Col. Chand. I tried to reason with her. 'We can't interfere in their family affairs unless they ask us to.'

A week later, Viju told me Colonel Chand had hit Raju with his DMS boot for not doing homework; he had broken Raju's finger. That same evening, I saw the father and son playing cricket in their garden. Raju's hand appeared to be in perfect condition. I lost my temper with Viju, and she retreated quietly into the kitchen.

Slowly, the stories stopped. Over the next few months, Viju started speaking less and less and sharing very little of her routine with me. Since I was busy with work, I did not pay much attention to it and was actually relieved that I did not have to hear horror stories about other people any more.

Then one day, I had to go to Vinayak's school alone because Viju was suffering from a bout of fever. This was the first time in a year that I attended the parent-teacher meet at our son's school—something that was almost always handled by Viju. I was surprised when the class teacher asked me to stay back till she was done with the other parents. She wanted to talk to me alone. I asked Vinayak if he had been in some trouble and was relieved when he assured me he hadn't. When we were the only ones in the class, the teacher sent Vinayak on an errand, which, I could easily make out, was an excuse to get him away.

'Why do you hit your wife and son?' she asked, as soon as we were alone. I was shocked. 'Mrs Krishnan has been telling me about your abusive behaviour. Last month you stuffed Vinayak's mouth with red chillies, because he had eaten too much at a party. It is unforgiveable,' she told me, her voice cold with suppressed anger. 'I would have reported it to the principal if Mrs Krishnan had not pleaded with me to keep it to myself. But really, Colonel Krishnan, I cannot tolerate this happening to my student. If I hear one more story about you, I shall report it. Strict action will be taken against you. I hope you are aware that the entire cantonment has heard stories about your abusive behaviour.'

Shocked and furious, I came home and confronted Viju. But, to my surprise, she appeared mortally afraid of me. She just cowered on her bed and whimpered, 'Don't hit me. I won't tell anyone anything again.' Her face was stained with tears. Much as I tried to convince her that I'd never ever raised my hand to her or Vinayak, she refused to believe me. The evil stories her mind was making up were real to her, and nothing I said or did could convince her that she was imagining it all.

•   Against her wishes, I took her to the hospital. The psychiatrist was frank with me: 'She is schizophrenic and will have to be on medication for life. I'm afraid it will slowly start getting worse. She might have to be institutionalized, Colonel Krishnan.'

It was an eventuality I was just not prepared to look at. With Vinayak, she was the perfect mother, loving, caring and affectionate. With me, she was mostly fine. But there were phases when she would keep away and avoid conversation. But she made up for this on the days she was well, and I could not imagine life without her. In fact, I kept her condition a secret not just from friends but from the family as well. She seemed normal in her interactions with her parents, and I did not want to worry them unnecessarily.

Over the past two months, she had been slipping steadily. She stopped taking phone calls on the landline, telling me that our phone was tapped. She would never answer the phone when I called the landline, always calling me back on the mobile, annoyed that I was being careless. I knew she needed to be hospitalized, but I just could not bring myself to take her there. I did not want to let go of Viju, selfishly. I just ensured that she took her medicines on time. But I could see that they were no longer as effective as they had been. The illness was slowly taking over her mind.

* * *

My breath was coming out in gasps now. The dull pain in my wrists was getting sharper. I no longer had the strength to lift my head, but I could see, out of the corner of my eye, that the blood stains were spreading further into the pale-blue bedsheet, colouring it a deep crimson.

'Viju,' I called out one more time, my voice a faint whisper. She jerked her head up, the blade still between her slim fingers. 'I will die, Viju. Is that what you want? Call Reddy. Take me to the hospital.'

She looked at me blankly and then, with surprise, at the gleaming blade in her hand, as if it was the first time she was seeing it. Her eyes rested on the two gold bangles on her wrist. They were a gift from her mother on our last wedding anniversary—the tenth. She touched them lovingly. Then, reaching out to Vinayak's study table, she picked up the wax paper the blade had come wrapped in. Snapping the blade in two, she folded the paper around one half of it, while with the other half she started sharpening a pencil that she had taken out of Vinayak's open geometry box. Sharpening it to a fine point, she placed the pencil back, keeping the blade next to it.

She dusted the pencil shavings off her lap and reached for her cell phone. Picking it up, she made a call. 'Hello, Amma,' she said softly. 'Amma, you have to book your flight tickets right now. Today I put sleeping pills in his tea. I have cut his wrists with a blade, Amma. I had to do it. He would have killed me and Vinayak.' She was crying softly.

Her light-brown eyes were covered with a film of tears that were slowly spilling over the corners of her eyes and slipping down her cheeks. 'Amma, come here by the next flight,' she said. 'How will I live without him?' Tears dripped off her eyelashes.

She looked at me. There was unfathomable emotion in her eyes. These were the same eyes I had fallen in love with twelve years back. 'Viju,' I whispered, gasping for breath. I wanted to coax her using the gentle-yet-firm tone she usually responded to, but the pain was getting unbearable. I couldn't speak any more.

Viju did not take her eyes off me. She picked up the bowl of biscuits and the mug with my leftover tea still in it from the bedside table. And then, smiling the same shy, hesitant smile that our son had inherited—which, at that moment, made me wonder if her condition was hereditary and if he would get it too—she got up and left the room, shutting the door firmly behind her.

'Bhaiya, sahab so rahe hain,' I heard her calling out to Reddy. 'Unko disturb nahi karna. Main Veenu ko tuition se le ke aati hun.'

Slipping in and out of consciousness, I heard the car start, reverse on the porch and leave. I heard Reddy opening and closing the heavy iron gate. I tried to call out to him, but my tongue had gone dry and was glued to my palate. I should not have kept her schizophrenia a secret. The doctor had been warning me it could get dangerous and had also told me to keep the Alprax out of Viju's reach. But it was too late for anything now. I shut my eyes in acceptance. The searing pain in my wrists was getting intolerable. My wrists were on fire. I just prayed that it would end soon.

* * *

Reddy had finished planting the bougainvillea hedge. He stood up to look at his work of the past hour in quiet satisfaction. All the cuttings were neatly spaced and planted, and he was sure the rain would ensure they took root quickly. Soon, there would be a beautiful hedge with magenta blossoms in place of the barbed-wire fence that separated the two neighbouring bungalows.

There was a deafening roll of thunder. He looked up to see a flash of lightning in the sky. It would rain soon, and he wanted to take Mastana for a run before that. He whistled to the dog, who was sprawled in the veranda, watching him from under his eyelashes. Reddy looked around for the leash. It lay near the main door. As he got there, he noticed that the main bedroom window was open. The mosquitoes would get in, he thought, clicking his tongue, and walked across to close the window . . .

* * *

And that was how I lived to tell you this tale, dear reader.

Subedar Major Negi Lays an Ambush

When Subedar Major Narendra Singh Negi, of 31 Garhwal Rifles, retired from service and came to settle down in the small riverside town of Kotdwar in Pauri Garhwal, he thought his career as a fighting soldier was over. He couldn't have been more mistaken.

Back then, he did not know that a covert operation was underway, and an unlikely enemy, who went by the name Rifleman Pancham Singh, also a retiree from the Garhwal Rifles from twenty years ago, was getting ready for an attack on his own comrade. Since Rifleman Pancham Singh happened to be from the same village as Mrs Negi, it earned him grandfather status from the Negi girls, both now settled abroad, who affectionately called him Five-Star Nanaji. Mrs Negi and Sub. Maj. Negi addressed him as Sipahi Chachaji, just like the rest of Kotdwar did. It was a mark of respect from the community for the services he had rendered to the nation.

Though nearing eighty, Sipahi Chachaji was as fit as the proverbial fiddle and way too gregarious for the reclusive Negi Sahab and his neighbour, the no-nonsense Brigadier Sahab who lived across the fence—civilian life having blurred all boundaries between officer-rank and other accommodations.

Sipahi Chachaji had unleashed terror in Kotdwar because of his penchant for walking uninvited into the homes of residents. Particularly at risk were those living on Badrinath Marg, the street leading to the sabzi mandi where he went to buy vegetables every day. Locals, who would be basking in the sun on their lawns, leapt inside their houses at the very sound of Sipahi Chachaji's lathi meeting the walkway, quite like the residents of Ramgarh village did at the sound of Gabbar Singh's boots in the epic film *Sholay*. But just like Gabbar, Sipahi Chachaji remained undeterred by this lack of welcome.

He would walk down Badrinath Marg in his old service Angola shirt, pleated trousers, Gandhi topi and Nehru jacket every morning, and if he noticed an open front door, he would take it as an invitation to visit and boldly walk in. Once he visited, he liked to stay for a while, regaling his nervous audience with disturbing tales about his piles, his pus-oozing molar, his indigestion, or, if they were more intellectually inclined, the political situation in the country. If the residents happened to be preoccupied with household work, he would indulge in a cover-to-cover read of their newspaper, sometimes slipping into a siesta in the sun, waking up only when a piping-hot cup of tea had been brought to him.

Badrinath Marg happened to be the street on which the unfortunate Sub. Maj. Negi had his sunshine-yellow bungalow, Vishranti, next door to the Brigadier's off-white one with its edges painted an elegant maroon, as a tribute to his career in the Parachute Regiment. Almost every other day, Sipahi Chachaji would amble expertly past the cows lurking outside Negi's house. He would push open the iron gate at the entrance, walk down the garden path and cough loudly outside their front door. Chutki, Negiji's black-and-white Lhasa Apso with buck teeth and a hairstyle reminiscent of Lady Gaga, would come running to greet him with a fallen leaf in her mouth as offering and perform a complicated tail-wag ritual that included a few body rolls on the grass. Giving her a tickle under the chin, Sipahi Chachaji would pull a grey plastic chair from the veranda and set it down under the mango tree, where the sunlight filtered through the dark-green leaves and fell upon his knees. And here he would sit with his eyes half-shut, ignoring Chutki and the lame squirrel that would climb down the tree and wait patiently, knowing that now it was just a matter of time before the food showed up.

In case his presence was not registered for a while, Sipahi Chachaji, who had also done a tenure as Drill Ustad in the Indian Military Academy at Dehradun, would take a deep breath, tighten his stomach muscles and bellow, '*Arre bhai, ghar mein koi hai?*' in a perfect example of '*pet se aawaaz nikalo, Mussorie tak sunai deni chahiye*'— the command he used to give to young gentlemen cadets on the parade ground back in the day. His call would send Sub. Maj. Negi, who hated these intrusions upon his privacy, scurrying to the safety of his bedroom from wherever in the house he happened to be. Mrs Negi would immediately appear, her shoulders respectfully covered with the pallu of her cotton sari, touch Sipahi Chachaji's feet with both hands and go in again to get him a cup of sweet milky tea and some biscuits. If he was lucky and the Negis' weekend guests had left behind some motichoor laddus, he would get to sample those as well.

Sub. Maj. Negi had intensely disliked Sipahi Chachaji's visits, right from that hot summer day twenty-two years ago, when Negi Sahab first stood under the mango tree at 1/37 Badrinath Marg, Upper Kalabarh, overseeing the construction of Vishranti on the plot of land gifted to him by his late father-in-law. But unlike the Brigadier, who'd moved next door to Negiji much later and who would just lock his door, refusing to open it to the unwanted guest even at persistent bell-ringing, Sub. Maj. Negi had been following the Gandhian philosophy of non-cooperation.

Usually, he wouldn't emerge from his bedroom till the old guest had left. If caught unawares—say, while soaking in the morning sun under the mango tree—he would pretend to have fallen asleep and obstinately refuse to respond when being spoken to. At which, Sipahi Chachaji would just slide the newspaper off Negi Sahab's lap and start reading it. While non-cooperation had worked fine with the British, it failed miserably in this case. Sipahi

Chachaji's attacks continued unabated, as did the food offerings made to him by Mrs Negi. So finally, the day after she had fed Sipahi Chachaji his favourite kaju katli, Sub. Maj. Negi decided to give up on his post-retirement allegiance to non-violence, resolving to pick up the weapons of destruction once again.

Now, very few people knew that, as a young boy, Sub. Maj. Negi had been a brilliant science student, who had harboured dreams of working with NASA until his father's sudden demise and the economic conditions of his family forced him to join the army as a soldier. But at heart, he had always remained a man of science. One afternoon, annoyed with the monkey horde that had been eating the perfectly ripened papayas from his tree, he built a small circuit and placed one end of the wire on the juiciest fruit. Every time, a monkey tried taking a bite of the papaya, it would get a nasty shock. The remedy worked like magic and soon Vishranti was rid of monkeys, who went off in search of less electrifying nourishment.

High on his recent success in animal trials, Sub. Maj. Negi decided to extend his experiment to mankind. Working stealthily when his wife was occupied with her morning puja (he expected human-rights protests from her), he fixed a similar circuit to the iron gate of his house and then waited in ambush behind the sitting-room curtains, his heart beating loudly. He had felt this kind of excitement once before, when during Operation Pawan in Sri Lanka his company had laid mines for the LTTE cadre around their camp and waited for them to attack. He could hardly concentrate on the *Dainik Jagran* in his hands, and his heart skipped a beat when he heard the familiar taps of the lathi on the road.

Peering from behind the curtain, he watched as Sipahi Chachaji reached out confidently for the gate and then quickly pulled his hand back in shock. Sipahi Chachaji tried to open the gate two more times and then, with a puzzled look on his face, went away, the taps of his walking stick slowly fading away. When Mrs Negi emerged from her bath, her wet hair rolled up in a towel, she found her husband innocently engrossed in the newspaper. 'Aaj Sipahi Chachaji nahi aaye?' she asked, at which he just shrugged.

The rest, as they say, is history. A visibly shaken Sipahi Chachaji was heard telling people at the chai ki dukan in Jhanda Chowk that the medicine he was taking for his piles seemed to have given him an electrical charge, which resulted in a shock every time he touched iron gates. When this news reached Sub. Maj. Narendra Singh Negi—through his incredulous wife, who'd heard it from Brigadier Sahab's incredulous wife, who'd heard it from the incredulous milkman—he just mumbled, 'Very strange!' and reached out for his plate of freshly diced papaya, a satisfied smile spreading across his face.

He spent the next morning under the mango tree at his favourite spot. Chutki lay loyally sprawled at his feet, chewing the edges of his sandals. That evening, Brigadier

Sahab, who too had heard the news from his wife, made an exception to his rule of not mingling socially with Other Ranks and came down to the fence to congratulate the victorious Subedar Major Sahab. A common enemy had been vanquished.

Home Alone

She shouldn't have gone for that jog so late in the evening. It was dark by the time she completed the circuit she routinely took. The end stretch was unnerving. The street lights went out suddenly, plunging the road in darkness, and she quickened her pace to a run, sprinting the last 200 metres to her house where, she hoped, the inverter-connected veranda light would be on. Army cantonments were considered safe. But then you never knew. It was stupid to take chances. 'Never again,' she whispered to herself, pushing open the iron gate to the driveway. The heady fragrance of the night jasmine wafted up her nostrils, and she let out a sigh of relief at the sight of the lone bulb outside the house, twinkling in the darkness. Unlocking the front door, she let herself in and stood on her toes to bolt it from the inside. Walking across to the fridge, she picked up a bottle of cold water and made her way to the bedroom, still panting from the strain of that last dash.

* * *

The tights she had just removed were lying on the floor beside the sneakers she had kicked off. She was peeling her sweat-wet T-shirt off when she noticed the shoes. Faded and slightly frayed, they were rust brown in colour and sticking out from beneath the thick beige curtains at the other end of the room. One of the pair had a rip darned with a white thread. Her blood froze. There was someone standing behind the drapes. She could make out the outline of a body from the way the fabric swelled slightly in places. The overhead light fell directly on the shoes.

She reached out for the cotton night shirt lying on the bed—she had planned to wear it after the bath—and pulled it over her head, her eyes glued to the intruder's shoes. She thought of shouting out for help, but fear made her voice stick in her throat. Even if she shouted, she knew, the chances of anyone hearing her in the old, secluded, British-time bungalow she lived in were slim. The neighbours were a hedge and two garages away. Even if they were to hear her screams, the man behind the curtain would reach her much before they would.

She wondered if he knew that she was all alone that weekend. Her husband was on a routine field firing eighty-five kilometres away and was to return the next day. Only this morning he had called to ask if she would like to send the boys to him, and she had readily agreed. They would return with their father, after an evening spent roasting fish and cooking Maggi on a bonfire at the lakeside where the battalion was camping. She had waved them goodbye a few hours back as they sat grinning happily in the jeep that had been sent to pick them up, jungle caps pulled low over the fauji crew cuts given to them by the unit barber, their backpacks stuffed with snacks and juice cartons. They were wearing identical T-shirts and shorts and were looking forward to meeting their dad, whom they hadn't seen for a week.

After the boys had left, she brewed herself a big mug of tea and went through the newspaper, enjoying the peace in the house. She had then decided to go for a jog, telling herself that she would fix herself a soup-and-sandwich dinner and spend a relaxed evening watching television, with a glass of Chardonnay. In the fifteen years that she had been married, she had stayed alone many times in areas much lonelier than General Cariappa Colony, but she had never been scared. In fact, she enjoyed the solitude.

At this moment, however, she was trembling with fear. Whether the person behind the curtain had been caught unawares by her entry and was just trying to hide or was waiting to attack her, she did not know. The bedroom door she had come in from was closer to him than to her, so she looked hopefully towards the bathroom, which was just a few feet away. If she managed to get in and lock the door from inside, she could escape into the garden from there . . . But the shoes moved suddenly, a hand darted for the light switch near the curtain, and the room was plunged into darkness.

She groped blindly for the bathroom door, but the figure had stumbled through the dark and now stood before her. She dropped to her knees and tried to crawl towards the bedside table, where the phone was kept. The last call had been made to her husband, and if only she could redial, he may be able to send help . . . Then all of a sudden, a strong and rough hand clasped her ankle and started dragging her back. She kicked hard, but her assailant was much stronger and managed to pull her back even as she screamed. Another hand closed around her mouth, fingers digging into her face. Her eyes bore into the darkness but she could see nothing.

* * *

She had been slipping in and out of consciousness. The pain in her throat was hot and searing—it eased only when the nurse injected a painkiller into the tube connected to her vein. She had received thirteen stitches on the neck. The surgeon said it was a miracle she had survived the vicious attack at all. The neighbours, a serving Colonel and his wife—on their way home from a dinner party—had heard her gasping from across the hedge and had come to check, thinking they would find an injured animal. They were shocked to see her lying in the driveway, her shirt soaked in blood, the breath wheezing out from the gash in her neck. The Colonel carried her to his car and, with his wife sitting beside her in the backseat, drove to the Base

Hospital. Then they called her husband. The doctors on emergency duty marvelled at her resilience and will to live.

The assailant had fled from an open window after slashing her neck with the dagger that hung as a decoration piece on their sitting-room wall. He had thrown the blood-stained weapon beside her motionless body, probably believing her to be dead. But not only had she willed herself to stay alive, she had also managed to drag herself to the front door, let herself out and even tried to walk towards the gate for help. Excessive blood loss made her collapse on the driveway.

* * *

Her husband pulled a chair close to the hospital bed on which she lay, with her head propped up on a soft pillow. Their older son was by his side. They were both looking at her with the same worried deep-brown eyes. She tried to smile and reached out for the little hand clutching the edge of the blanket covering her. The boy was nearly ten and already seemed on the verge of becoming a handsome man, just like his father. He let her hold his hand and bravely fought the quiver of his lip.

Behind the father and the son was a familiar figure: Brijender, her husband's man Friday who had been with them for ten years and was now a trusted member of the family. His eyes were clouded with tears, and he held in his arms her younger son, who was clutching a shiny red

Hot Wheels car. It was a toy she hadn't seen before, so she guessed it was a bribe for staying at home with Bhaiya while Daddy spent the nights at the hospital with Mamma. She beckoned to the child to come to her, but he buried his face in Brijender's neck, sobbing loudly. The strange woman with the tubes sticking into her arms and nose and with bandages wrapped around her neck did not look like the happy, smiling mother he knew.

'Take the children home, Brijender. Their dinner will come from the mess. Sleep in their room. I'll come back in the morning,' her husband was saying, leaning his head back wearily on the chair he was sitting on. Brijender nodded and straightened briskly to say, 'Ram Ram, sa'ab.'

His sudden movement made the red car slip out of the child's clammy hand. It fell on the floor with a metallic thump. Her eyes followed the toy and stopped at the pair of faded rust-brown canvas shoes—one of them had a rip on its side darned with a dirty-white cobbler's thread. Brijender bent down to pick up the toy, wiped it on his shirt and handed it to the little one in his other arm. She watched him as he took the older boy by the hand and they began to walk towards the door. She whispered, 'Stop him.' Her husband raised his head in surprise. Her breath was coming out in painful gasps, her skin had erupted in goose pimples. 'Stop him,' she said hoarsely. 'I have seen those shoes before.'

Munni Mausi*

The house Radhika lived in had a bamboo door. The floor, however, was mud, which made it difficult to spot the occasional snake that would slither in with the monsoon rain, slipping past the wire mesh on the kitchen drain.

Radhika loved the feel of the earthen floor under her toes, but she was not walking barefoot any more. So much had changed after Munni Mausi died. The snakes had their burrows flooded with water. The baby had started kicking inside her belly. And Manoj had walked for five days to reach his post at Tame Chung Chung, the Mountain of Poisonous Snakes, from where he had not returned yet.

Alone in her bamboo home, Radhika would spend the days retching into the sink and the nights listening for the tap on the window, which meant Munni Mausi had her face pressed against the thin glass and was trying to get in.

---

* An abridged version of this story was among the winning entries at the 2008–09 Commonwealth Short Story Competition.

Radhika would shut her eyes tight, place her hand on her tummy to feel the baby moving inside and turn her back to the aunt she had loved all her life.

She had stopped using the toilet after dark, scared that she would walk into Munni Mausi, with her plump legs straddling the white commode, her ikat print cotton nightie hitched up, her grey hair untidily bunched at the neck. Instead, Radhika would cradle her big, bulging stomach, contract her pelvic muscles and wait for morning to empty the bladder that seemed about to burst. She would slip a hand under her pillow and find the tiny silver cross, attached to a string of rosary beads, that nestled there. How would another religion protect her when all thirty-three crore of her own gods and goddesses could not? She didn't know, but the rosary, given to her by a young Assam Rifles officer on his way back home after three years in the jungles of Arunachal, instilled in her a desperate faith that all these years of lighting incense sticks hadn't been able to.

She would think of the baby that was going to come after two years of painful infertility treatment—operations to unblock a closed fallopian tube, monthly ovulation monitoring, ultrasounds on full bladder, the indignity of having her legs spread wide and cryopreserved semen shot into her with an injection that she felt would kill her with disgust if not discomfort someday. And Munni Mausi by her side. In her starched cotton sari. Driving her to the hospital, slipping the keys into her red leather purse after locking the car, handing her the large, brown paper envelope with the earlier reports and ultrasounds, cracking jokes to ease the anxiety, telling her that if nothing worked there was always adoption.

And, kulfi-falooda! They would laugh and walk down to the pavement bookseller in the evening to peer at *Fantasy*, Delhi's bold new magazine with semi-nude pictures and quirky letters sent in by readers. They would giggle like teenagers, remembering the day Munni Mausi had asked the boy for a copy, and he had taken one look at her plump frame, her cotton salwar kameez, her white hair and spectacles and whispered conspiratorially, 'Auntiji rehne do. Ye aapke matlab ki kitaab nahi hai.'

Her first cone from an ice-cream parlour, her first salami, her first dress from London (a gift from Munni Mausi's first trip abroad), that first nervous day in journalism class, even the first boyfriend (who came riding a motorbike and left soon after the romance was callously terminated by Munni Mausi with the threat, 'If I see him again, I will tell your parents')—a lifetime's worth of wistful memories would flood her mind as she spent her nights wide awake, her eyes squeezed shut. They would take her to places she hadn't visited in a while.

* * *

It was a navy-blue A-line frock, with a cream-coloured hand-embroidered panel around the neck. Radhika would want to wear it to every single birthday party she was invited to. And when someone asked her where she had got it from, she would look down shyly and whisper, 'Foreign ki hai.'

Back in those days, she lived in the small, faded town of Agra, where Mughal emperors once ruled and had left behind hypnotically beautiful ruins for ages to come. Radhika knew only three other countries besides India—America (where Archie and Veronica lived); Japan (where people with narrow eyes lived and ate noodles with chopsticks); and lately, London (where Munni Mausi had gone and got her the blue dress from).

Munni Mausi had been the first woman in the family to do a lot of unusual things, like moving to Delhi and getting herself a proper job, living alone in a flat, learning to drive a car, not getting married and having a best friend who was a man. She was also the first in the family to get on an Air India plane and fly abroad for work.

Radhika had been a small, thin kid back then, with her skin a shade darker than was considered pretty by Indian standards. She would go to school with her hair braided in two, long, well-oiled plaits, bound securely by red ribbons knotted into perfectly symmetrical flowers by her mom. She was painfully shy, didn't have many friends, wouldn't speak unless she was spoken to and could never go to her class teacher to complain that the boy who sat behind her sometimes pulled her hair.

She continued to hate school even after she'd moved to an all-girls convent, where the girls slyly rolled up their skirts from the waistband to make them shorter, and the boy who had pulled her hair was no longer around to bother her. The only time she remembered laughing was when the mousy 'Chuah Sir'—her physics teacher, Mr Chauhan—with his neatly combed, side-parted black hair and pencil moustache, stood up in the middle of the class and said, rather sternly, that he wanted all the girls to come to his desk one by one and show him their 'figures'. He was referring to a diagram he had given out for homework. The sound of Munni Mausi laughing heartily at that story could still bring a smile to Radhika's face.

* * *

She was fourteen when a road accident left her on a wheelchair and then put her on crutches for almost a year, until she was able to walk again. She had a long surgical scar running down one leg and an ugly patch of mangled skin at the ankle that she had to wear socks to hide. Her body had a tendency to form keloids—big, ugly scars. The surgeon had told her that plastic surgery could help, but after three major surgeries and nearly two years in hospitals, she didn't have the courage left for another operation.

That was the time when Munni Mausi had come visiting and told her that scars were not important, songs were. She helped Radhika find Masterji, a friendly Indian classical music teacher, who had a few teeth missing, spoke with a lisp and came riding a sputtering old green Bajaj scooter. But when he sat with his legs crossed into an althi-palthi and sent his plump fingers flying over the black and white keys of his harmonium, he could create magic. Rich musical notes would fill the air as his rings flashed in the sunlight, and Radhika would slip into a trance, where ugly scars no longer mattered.

Masterji introduced her to raga Yaman, with its teevra 'ma'; to the haunting 'Jab Deep Jale Aana'; to the deep, throaty Bhairav, with the komal 're' and 'dha' that always made the mood sombre; and to the effervescent Des, which brought with it the patter of raindrops on green leaves and the mesmerizing smell of moist earth. The music had stayed with her long after Masterji left.

When she finished college and was aimlessly wondering about what to do next with life, she was invited to Delhi by Munni Mausi and was coaxed into joining a journalism class.

'I think you should write,' Munni Mausi had said one warm summer afternoon, putting her newspaper aside, her granny glasses balanced on the tip of her nose, her cotton sari crushed as she lay sprawled on the bed, propped up against one fat and one thin semal-ki-rui-wali pillows.

'Write what, Mausi?' Radhika asked, taking a bite of the apple she had got from the fridge.

'Stories,' her aunt suggested airily.

Stories are born in the heart—from seeds quietly sown by people who once walked in and out of it—and can only be written when they start to choke you with their weight. You can write a story only when there is one inside you, asking to be written; when the eyes are moist and the fingers are ready to type with muscle memory that does not involve the mind, giving it time to put floating, fleeting, abstract thoughts into words. You can't just sit down one fine day and start writing a story. That's what she could have told Munni Mausi now—after almost twenty years of writing—but she did not know it then. She had just kept quiet and gone to the sitting room, where books by T.S. Eliot, Harivansh Rai Bachchan, Bertrand Russel and authors as different from each other as Premchand and P.G. Wodehouse were stacked together in a small alcove behind the door.

* * *

Soon, Radhika got a job at a newspaper, where the newsroom was dominated by bearded JNU dropouts, with communist mindsets and shockingly colourful vocabularies; bright Bihari graduates who hadn't been able to clear their Civil Services interviews; and pompous Bengali intellectuals, wearing khadi kurtas and an air of cultural superiority. There, she met Ashu, the swashbuckling crime reporter, who called her Beautiful Smile and tossed her his reports to edit whenever he went out to have a smoke and a sandwich. She tried to stay out of the way of the gorgeous but sharp-tongued Padmini, who would sweep into the subs room and, with a tilt of her head and a swish of her long skirt, made even old Mr Bhattacharya, the chief sub editor, look up and wait for his turn to be rewarded with a smile.

Radhika made friends with the romantic Jatin, who fell in love with each new secretary the editor employed but considered Radhika the backslapping buddy he could share work, heartbreak and Nirula's chocolate-chip ice cream with during that phase between two romances, when he wore a stubble and scowled at the world. Five years passed as she changed jobs, learnt to make new friends, acquired life skills and found the courage to reach out to strangers and talk.

But the best part of her life in those days as well was the time she spent with Munni Mausi. On weekends, there were Bhimsen Joshi concerts at Kamani Auditorium; plays by the National School of Drama students at Shri Ram Centre; visits to the florist at Connaught Place to pick up fragrant tube roses at rupees five a stem. There were golgappa treats at Bengali Market; crisp Mysore masala dosas at Sagar Ratna in Defence Colony; home-cooked curd rice, with a tadka of mustard seeds and curry leaves cooled in the fridge, at C-502, Curzon Road Apartments.

There were lazy walks with Kala Moti, Munni Mausi's black Lhasa apso. There were jokes about Sonu, who lived on the upper floor and whose clothes dropped mysteriously on to the balcony every time Radhika came to Munni Mausi's apartment for an overnight stay. He would soon show up at the front door to pick up the clothes, politely ringing the doorbell just once. 'I think he finds excuses to come here because he likes me.' Munni Mausi would laugh while Radhika would blush and bury her head in her book.

There were train journeys to the old family home in Kotdwar, where a print of Georges Seurat's *Bathers at Asnières* (brought back from the same London trip) hung in Munni Mausi's bedroom, its window overlooking the temple of Sidhbali, perched midway up a green hill, where bhajans rang out and bells chimed early in the morning. There were afternoons they spent sprawled on the sofa, reading Ghalib's poetry; evenings made richer by dipping crisp samosa edges in spicy green chutney; and nights when they both sat in the veranda and sang, watching a lazy yellow moon flirt halfheartedly with the stars. Yaman and Bihag and Bageshwari; the flirtatious 'Shola Jo Bhadke, Dil Mera Dhadke'; and the soulful 'Man Tarpat Hari Darshan Ko Aaj', which Radhika could never sing again after Munni Mausi died, because it made her throat choke and her eyes brim with tears.

* * *

At work, Radhika had moved on and had started enjoying a career she had picked up just by chance. And then one day, she gave it all up for a handsome young army officer with gentle brown eyes and crew-cut hair. She had first noticed him looking at her from across the hall at a family wedding in Dehradun. He had managed to trace her hostel address and began to woo her with romantic cards—there would be one waiting for her in the Working Women's Hostel mailbox every evening she got back from work, and two on Mondays, since the postman did not visit on Sundays. This went on for nearly a year, with him calling her occasionally, though never prodding for a concrete reply.

She left journalism and Delhi for a place called Kimin in Arunachal Pradesh, where her husband was deputed with the Assam Rifles and where there was no Internet or electricity, only unending grey rain and tall grass where snakes slithered out of flooded burrows and often entered bamboo homes. For this reason, the tribals lived in huts built on stilts, with pigs squealing from makeshift sties underneath.

The most interesting part of her evening was spent watching the local kids, with their fat, pink cheeks and shiny black eyes, huddle around the street light in the army cantonment (powered by a generator till ten each night). The kids came here to gather insects, which they took home in transparent polythene bags and which their mothers fried for a crunchy snack to go with a candlelit dinner of salt and rice.

Her husband soon left her for a stint at Tame Chung Chung on the China border, where telephone connectivity was so bad that she couldn't speak to him more than twice a month. When she discovered that she was pregnant, she had to wait twelve days to tell him the good news, till she finally got him on the walkie-talkie. The line crackled and buzzed incessantly, and he said, 'What?' so many times that at the end of that tedious conversation she wasn't even sure if he had understood what she was trying to tell him. So she finally swallowed her modesty and told the soldier manning the exchange that she was pregnant and asked him to please pass on the news to 'sahab'. 'Bahut achhi khabar hai, memsahab,' the soldier had replied with so much warmth that it brought a lump to her throat.

* * *

Life became a little difficult after that. She spent the days puking into the bathroom sink and nights holding her belly, which seemed to be growing each day. And then, one evening, Radhika got a call informing her that Munni Mausi was no more, having silently collapsed after a heart attack in an autorickshaw; she had felt some discomfort in her chest and was en route to the hospital. Since she was diabetic, it would not have hurt much, was what Munni Mausi's lifelong friend, Sharma Uncle, had told Radhika, who was relieved to know that he had been by Munni Mausi's side when she breathed her last.

Radhika went to the kitchen and took out from the creaky wooden cupboard the set of exquisitely cut crystal glasses that had been a wedding gift from Munni Mausi—used only when someone special came over for dinner. She filled a goblet with water and sat down with it on the steps outside her hut, a smoking mosquito repellant coil by her side. She quietly watched the dark clouds sieve the fading sunlight and the rain fall over the mountains that her husband had crossed. He was so far from her—just when she had needed him the most.

She went inside only after the kids, who had gathered around the streetlight, started making their way back to their homes with noisy chatter, which meant it was going to be lights out soon. She locked the door after a routine check behind the curtains and beneath the bed, a steel rod clasped tightly in one hand. Then she made herself a cucumber sandwich and some tea and curled up in her bed to sleep. That was the first night there had been a knock on the window.

* * *

Munni Mausi was lonely, in need for company, and had come looking for Radhika thousands of miles from Delhi, with her delicate, brown hands with oval nails and two gold bangles, trying to unlatch the bedroom window. The nocturnal visits, the loo sharing, the clattering pans in the kitchen (Munni Mausi cooking her sour buttermilk kadhi) were slowly driving Radhika mad.

Sometimes, she would hear utensils clanking in the kitchen, sometimes the flush turning, sometimes a swish of starched cotton or a whiff of Chanel No. 5, Munni Mausi's favourite perfume that Radhika easily recognized. She was being haunted by the aunt she had loved all her life. The evil, constricting fear that parched her skin, made her throat go dry and made her a nervous wreck as night approached, stayed with her for more than a month, till she thought she would asphyxiate in its suffocating hold.

This haunting had to end, Radhika decided one day, looking into the bathroom mirror, her fingers moving over her sunken cheeks and papery yellow skin. She thought she could see behind her a reflection of a grey-haired woman and bit her lip to stifle a scream. When the tap came on the window that night, Radhika lifted herself off the bed, walked across to the window and, parting the curtains, stared into the darkness. There was nothing there. She returned to the bed and leant back on her pillow.

That night, she shut her eyes and took the black-and-yellow autorickshaw from outside her Working Women's Hostel on Bhagwandas Road, as she had done almost every weekend for seven years, when she worked as a journalist. She revisited the house where tube roses rested in a terracotta vase and Kala Moti looked up through his fringe, growling from under the teak takht. She stepped on the green handloom durrie she had once helped select at Dilli Haat and ran her hand over the coarse yellow floor cushion she had sunk into so many times. She heard the curry leaves crackling in the kadahi in the kitchen, saw the crushed newspaper on the bed, the reading glasses beside it and the hairpins on the side table.

She looked in the lift, the lawns where mogra flowers bloomed and among the vendors selling fat, red slices of papaya on the street corner. She entered the corner bookshop, walked over to the 'Indian Authors' rack, where the Upamanyu Chatterjees were kept, and finally, she sat down on a wooden stool, her hands folded in her lap, tears streaming down her cheeks. She wept loudly, for a time that would never come back, for someone she would never be able to touch again, for a voice she would never hear, for hands she would never again hold.

And once the sobs had abated and the tears had run dry, she lifted her head. 'I'm at peace, Radhika,' she heard Munni Mausi say. 'Let me go.'

Radhika looked up to see her holding two fat books in her hand and gazing down at her with affection in her eyes. She saw Munni Mausi turn and walk away.

Radhika brushed the tears off her eyelashes, turned the pillow around to keep her head off the wet fabric and slept undisturbed for the first time after many nights.

* * *

The next morning, she made herself a mug of tea, rubbed some smelly, yellow Odomos on the bare skin of her legs and arms and sat on the steps in front of her house with a pencil and an old diary.

Over the months, she slowly realized that when she wrote, she stepped into a world where there was no anger or sadness or hurt about people who did and scars that didn't go away. She had found a space where all her fears and inhibitions vanished and found the power to stretch her imagination and take what she wanted, give what she wanted, touch raw emotion and convert it into typed text. She learnt how stories were written.

* * *

A few years later, a journalism fellowship took her to London, and she went a little apprehensively, leaving her three-year-old son in his father's care. 'London is not a country,' she whispered to herself when she got off the plane at Heathrow Airport, wheeling her cabin bag behind her.

On her first free afternoon, Radhika took the tube to Charing Cross and walked down to Trafalgar Square, where children were splashing in the fountain and clambering over the lions for a picture. She walked up the steps of the National Gallery, asked for a map and found her way to the Impressionists section, where she spent some time gazing at Van Gogh's *Sunflowers*. And then she found what she had been trying to find all along. The magnificent *Bathers at Asnières,* oil-on-canvas, hung on an almost bare wall. She waited for her turn to sit on the bench facing the painting and sat there soaking in its ethereal beauty, just as Munni Mausi had once probably done. Radhika was finally at peace with herself . . .

Guruji

'Will all those who have not done their homework please stand up?' said Naithaniji in his deep, gravelly voice.

A wave of cold terror ran down young Murli Prasad's back. Not only had he not done his homework, he also did not know how to say that in English, which, he knew from experience, was going to be Guruji's next request. He was right.

'Those standing will now tell me why they haven't completed their homework.' Guruji's voice was cold, and he was menacingly stroking the thin cane in his hand.

It was a time to test friendships. While Guruji turned his back to the class, to spit the remains of the betel nut in his mouth into the dustbin next to the blackboard, Murli whispered urgently to Ajay sitting next to him. 'Batha, jaldi batha,' he mumbled in his sing-song Garhwali accent, 'homework nahin kiya ko angreji mein kya kehte hain bal?'

'I did not do my homework,' Ajay whispered back, keeping his head cunningly bent over his textbook, so that the movement of his lips was invisible to the world.

Wiping his running nose with the back of his frayed sweater sleeve, Murli pretended to be deeply engrossed in rummaging inside his school bag. A smart move, since Guruji had turned to face the class again and was using the edge of his palm to clear his white moustache of the fine sprinkling of chewed supari deposited there.

'Yes, Murli?' he asked, prowling around Murli's desk like a tiger in the forest, cane dangling casually from one hand, trailing an invisible path behind him as he walked.

Murli hesitantly stood up. His lowered eyes were following the movement of the cane, and he was getting more and more nervous as it came closer. He and his mother had only recently come to live in Jaiharikhal, a small town in Pauri Garhwal, to be with his father, who was a soldier in the Garhwal Rifles.

Back in the village, everyone spoke Garhwali. Murli had never learnt to speak English, though he could write the English alphabet and do the 'A for *apil, apil mane seb*; B for *bwaay, bwaay mane ladka*' routine fairly well if there was a picture book at hand. But speaking full sentences was a formidable task.

Naithaniji halted in front of Murli's seat and was looking down at him with his spectacles glinting, his voice dangerously mellow. 'Murli?' He was awaiting an answer.

Murli froze in fear. 'I d-d-d . . . I do not did my homework . . .' he mumbled, trying desperately to remember the sequence of the words Ajay had told him. There was a quick swish in the air and the cane had landed on his bottom even before he could finish his sentence. He whimpered softly, his hands rubbing the spot where it felt as if his butt had been set on fire.

'Arre gawaron. Tum karoge angrezon ki barabari? You squat on stones to shit. You think you will ever speak English? Do you know that the English shit sitting on chairs?' a furious Naithaniji growled, shaking his head gravely. Then, much to Murli's relief, he popped some more supari into his mouth and moved ahead.

Murli sat down and as soon as Naithaniji was at a safe distance, he got into a hushed discussion with Ajay about what the toilets of the English might look like and how difficult it must be to shit while sitting on a chair.

Leaving aside English lessons, Murli was enjoying school. The boys were rosy-cheeked and friendly and often came to class in slippers and pyjamas which made Murli feel quite at home. That their mothers had washed their grey school trousers which had not yet dried was a good enough excuse to not be in uniform. Jaiharikhal was a cold place, and Guruji knew that none of the families could afford to get more than one pair of trousers stitched for their children. So as long as you had some piece of your uniform in place, no punishments were meted out.

While some of the boys wore pyjamas with school shirts, ties and sweaters, others teamed uniform pants with multi-coloured, hand-knit pullovers. Some even came wearing their older siblings' footwear, either having broken the straps of their own slippers playing football or not being able to find one of the pair in a hurry to get to school before the assembly bell rang. Many of the girls wore skirts with hemlines extended term after term, the faded stitch marks showing just how much taller they had grown.

While Guruji got very upset with incorrect English, he was quite understanding about shabby dressing. You could even say that he endorsed it. Often, he would himself come to teach in a pullover that was unravelling from the back, where he had caught it on a loose nail sticking out of his straight-backed wooden chair in the class. In fact, most of Naithaniji's clothes had a rip at the back, which was a sort of indication that he taught Class Five.

Whatever his animosity towards the English language and Guruji's cane, Murli bore no malice towards his teacher. In fact, since he himself did not have too many clothes, he was quite sympathetic towards Naithaniji's ripped sweaters. One day, he decided to put an end to the nail saga. He got hold of the heavy class duster, with the fat wooden base and a green sponge at the top, and was in the process of hammering the wicked nail sticking out of the class teacher's chair when Naithaniji walked in and caught him by the ear, suspecting that he was up to some tricks.

Murli was too tongue-tied to explain what he was doing (he also could not say it in English). But Ajay got up and explained Murli's attempted good deed, making Naithaniji take off his sweater to show him the tear the nail had made.

'Thank you, my boy,' a visibly touched Naithaniji said to Murli, letting go of the ear he was holding between his fingers in a pincer-like grip. 'I'm sorry I misunderstood you.'

'Menshun naat, Guruji,' Murli declared, blushing as pink as the tip of his pinched ear.

'Not. Pronounce that like you pronounce "hot",' said Guruji, correcting him gently. This was the first time Naithaniji had smiled at him.

For Murli, it was as if the sun had emerged from behind the clouds and was sending its warm rays in through the open window, to where he stood, next to his English teacher, blushing darkly on that chilly winter day.

Thereafter, Murli started liking his English classes. He learnt that instead of 'My come in, sir' he had to say, 'May I come in, sir'. What he thought was 'omelette' was in fact 'I am late'. And if he rephrased 'May I do toilet?' just a little bit and asked 'May I go to the toilet?' instead, it made Naithaniji so much happier.

On his way to school, a five-kilometre walk from his house, Murli would sometimes catch from afar, at the turn of the road, the maroon of Naithaniji's pullover. He would sling his bag across his back, sprint along the hillside and clamber up the slopes, getting wisps of fern and fallen pine leaves caught in his hair.

Breathless and red-nosed from the early morning run in the cold, he would catch up with his English teacher and cheerfully greet him with 'Namaste, Guruji', adding a 'Good Morning, Sir' for good measure. The two would then walk together in companionable silence, listening to the rustle of the wind up in the pine trees and the piercing call of the hill bird, from somewhere deep inside the thicket, that sounded like the bird was saying *'kafal pako, mil ni chakho'*—the kafal fruit has ripened but I didn't taste it. They would watch the white-flecked whistling thrush hop across the track and the snow-covered Dhauladhar range far in the distance, changing colour in the sunlight on a clear day.

Sometimes, Murli would pick up ferns with spore-whitened undersides from the road and stamp them on his wrist, making Christmas trees on his dry skin even as Guruji stood smiling. And sometimes, they would come upon a patch of wild daisies, and Murli would point them out because he had come to love the verse Guruji would break into:

'I wandered lonely as a cloud
That floats on high o'er vales and hills,
When all at once I saw a crowd,
A host, of golden daffodils . . .'

Murli did not know what daffodils looked like, and when he asked Guruji, it turned out he didn't either. 'They grow in England, Murli. Maybe when you grow up, you will go there and see them some day. I know I never will. But that doesn't matter, I'm sure they are as pretty as the yellow marigolds we have growing in our town.'

Murli would nod obediently.

* * *

Many years had passed. Murli had left Jaiharikhal to move with his father, studied in various army cantonments, completed his graduation and, after clearing his Civil Services exams and interview (in English), he had joined the Indian Foreign Service.

His first posting was in the UK. After the Air India flight landed at Heathrow, he watched pigeons strutting casually down the airfield, completely unconcerned about the planes. He was amazed by the Indian faces he encountered at the airport and particularly drawn by an old man seated on a wheelchair. The man had a stark white beard, wore a white kurta pyjama and shawl and looked intently at Murli while being wheeled away. His eyes seemed to bore right into Murli's soul, but it was his feet that caught his attention. Bare, brown, long-toed, they were frail and finely veined, and he had them stretched elegantly over the footrest of the wheelchair. It was only after he had been taken away that a bell rang in Murli's head. 'M.F. Husain! That was M.F. Husain,' he blurted out loud, startling an English lady standing next to him, waiting for her luggage on the conveyor belt.

Murli took a cab to Birmingham, which happened to
be the location for his first foreign posting. He took a few
days to settle down in the beautiful duplex house he had
been given. He learnt how to segregate waste into different
coloured bags, how to switch the central heating on and
off and how to use his pressure cooker without setting off
the fire alarm.

A few days later, after he had opened most of his
luggage, he decided to explore the area around Edgbaston
Reservoir, which was walking distance from his house.
Strolling thoughtfully around the sparkling lake, watching
joggers in shorts and fathers with chattering kids, he came
across a clutch of golden yellow flowers growing along
its bank. Next to them was a signboard that read: 'Please
don't pluck daffodils.' Murli stared at the sign and then at
the flowers for what seemed like an eternity.

He looked beyond the still blue waters to the narrow
mud track that turned along the edge of the lake. He
thought he could see a man with a familiar shuffling walk,
wearing an old, maroon pullover, with the rip in its back
darned with a thread of a different colour. If he could,
Murli would have run after that fading figure and pulled
at his elbow, where the sleeve sagged a bit. He would have
brought him all the way to where he was now standing
and pointed out the flowers that seemed to be smiling
cheerfully in the afternoon sun.

But instead, Murli took off his spectacles and blinked
to clear the wetness in his eyes that was blurring his vision.

'Look, Guruji, daffodils,' he said, gently reaching out to touch a yellow petal.

Naithaniji had passed away many years ago, making his final journey in a bier lifted by his sons. There had been yellow marigold flowers scattered on the white sheet covering his body.

Hearts and Minds

It was 5 a.m. when the nearly six and a half feet tall and intimidating Subedar Bhim Singh Raizada stormed into Company Commander Major Somnath Batabyal's office. Batabyal, or Bat Ball, and his company 2IC (second-in-command) Captain Amit Dogra, had been up all night, waiting for reports from the section of thirty-two soldiers led by Raizada that had surrounded a nearby village. The unit had received intelligence that two armed militants had taken shelter in a house there, and Bat Ball was expecting a major arrest. But one look at Raizada's face told him that he was not going to hear any good news.

'SHO Sa'ab ne iss baar bhi hamare saath aadmi bhejne se mana kar diya, sahab,' growled Raizada. Still in army fatigues and bulletproof vest, he was holding his helmet in his hands and fuming in frustration. 'We would have caught the rebels by the scruff of their necks, but all our hard work was in vain. The cordon-and-search operation had to be called off.'

Batabyal leant back in his chair, his dark curls falling untidily on his forehead, and ran a hand through his overgrown beard, scowling darkly at nothing in particular. He and most of his men had grown their hair and beards and had started wearing phirans in place of uniforms because they often worked incognito. The government rule that the army could not search a village without the presence of local police representatives had become a big problem for them ever since the new SHO had taken over the police station in their area. Dogra, also in a phiran, was chewing on his fingernails, which Bat Ball looked at as a good sign, because it meant that the evil 'Doggy' mind was ticking.

This was the second time in the month that a cordon-and-search operation had to be called off. 'Every time we ask SHO Sa'ab to send his men with us, he says he cannot spare people at such short notice,' Raizada, who had been in the jungle all night with his men, said angrily. 'The assistant sub-inspector at the police chowki told me that SHO Sa'ab has hated the army ever since he was rejected by the Service Selection Board interview panel. It was his dream to join the army but he couldn't.'

'Army ne us ko nahi liya toh wo hamari le raha hai? Bahut na-insaafi hai,' Bat Ball murmured. 'Kuch toh karna padega.' He looked expectantly at Dogra, whose eyes were glinting darkly behind his spectacles as he shuffled nervously on his feet. 'Why don't you sit down, Doggy? You will think better,' Bat Ball said, pointing to the chair placed in front of him.

Doggy ignored the offer. Pulling his lower lip into a pout, which made him look like a human goldfish, Doggy said an idea was being formed in his great mind. Both Raizada and Bat Ball retreated into respectful silence. 'OK, sir! I got it,' Doggy declared, bending his head closer to his Company Commander's and lowering his voice to a whisper, which forced Raizada to lean in all the way to get closer to the conspiring mastermind.

At the end of Dogra's short but succinct monologue, intercepted only by Batabyal's emotional 'Shabash Doggy!' and Raizada's 'Kya dimaag paya hai, sa'ab', the mood in the Company Commander's office had changed completely. Bat Ball was looking at Doggy with a benevolent Bhagwan Vishnu-looking-at-his-favourite-bhakt kind of smile. Dogra had puffed up his chest and looked like a proud penguin in a phiran. Raizada wore an expression of gleeful evil that made his dark, menacing face appear even scarier than usual.

The party broke off for breakfast, and the three of them enjoyed the langar's crisp puris with spicy aloo sabzi, washing them down with mugs of piping-hot chai—Raizada with his men in the cookhouse; Doggy and Bat Ball sitting across from each other in the Company Commander's office.

* * *

That night, Rafiq Ahmad Dar, SHO of Larnu Police Chowki, South Kashmir, had his usual two large pegs of rum and a chicken curry-with-chapati dinner. He then changed into his flannel pyjamas and had just got inside his blanket with a hot-water bottle tucked under his feet when he thought he heard firing outside.

It was probably that chutiya Major Batabyal making his men do some night firing practice, he thought to himself and, pulling a pillow over his head, closed his eyes, his toes resting on the comforting hot-water bottle. But then, the firing got louder and sounded alarmingly close to the police chowki.

Dar got out of bed and had just parted his bedroom curtains when two grenades seemed to land right outside the police station and exploded, leaving a cloud of thick grey smoke. Startled, he called up the Duty Constable, who too seemed to have just woken up. 'Sahab, chowki pe militant attack ho raha hai!' he shrieked, making a shiver run down Rafiq's spine.

'Stay inside! Fire from the windows,' Dar yelled, running to the sitting room of his two-room living quarters, which was just a furlong away from the police station. Looking out of the sitting-room window, he could clearly make out three shadowy figures under the only streetlight in that area. They were across the road from the police station and firing indiscriminately. Dar stood there wrapped in the window curtain, watching them silently, with his bare feet freezing on the cemented floor.

After about ten minutes of intermittent firing, which was answered by retaliatory fire from the police station, the three men—dressed in phirans, their faces covered with scarves and AK-47s in their hands—started raising slogans of 'Allah-hu-Akbar' and 'Jaish zindabad'. Flinging a few more grenades inside the police station compound, they turned around and ran across the road, retreating into the dense forest.

Dar quickly threw a thick jacket over his night suit, slipped his feet into his boots, reached out for his rifle and dashed across to the police station. The two constables on night duty were cowering around the SHO's table, their scared faces reflected in the light of the bukhari burning inside. They told him they had not seen anything more than he had. The three attackers had apparently emerged from inside the forest and disappeared back into it. 'Jaish militants, sahab,' the constables told Dar. 'One of them was definitely a big, towering Afghan.'

* * *

The next morning, at around 11, Bat Ball was sitting in his office, eating hot sevai. He was still smarting from the morning conference call with his commanding officer, Colonel Jang Bir Singh, Vir Chakra, who, not without reason, was known as Krur Singh. He had not minced his words telling Batabyal exactly what he thought of a Company Commander with two botched-up cordon-and-search operations in a month. Batabyal's whiney excuses

that the police had not cooperated did not cut any ice
with him.

'You bloody idiots! This is a battle of hearts and minds.
It's time you assholes stopped behaving like gun-toting
Robin Hoods. You turn people off with your arrogance. I
am warning you—alter your behaviour. Show people you
care. The local police have to become your friend. Win
them over with love and affection. Win their hearts and
minds,' Krur Singh had roared, making Bat Ball move the
radio set away from his ear, mouthing 'Buddha bidak gaya
hai' to a grim Dogra who was silently shaking his head.

The CO had finally signed off with a menacing, 'I
had better see some results from your area. I am disgusted
with you. Out!' rudely cutting Bat Ball off in the middle
of his whimpering, 'Sir, it's the new SHO who is creating
trouble . . .'

'Sahab, Larnu Police Chowki ke SHO Sahab aaye
hain,' Batabyal's runner peeped in to inform him.

'Bring him in,' he responded, tilting the bowl of sevai
to pour the last of it straight into his open mouth and
wiping his lips with the back of his phiran sleeve.

A tall, fair and good-looking man, Sub-inspector Rafiq
Ahmad Dar walked in with a cardboard carton in his hands.
Batabyal rose from the chair and stepped forward to shake
hands with him. 'Oye, SHO Sahab ke liye sevai lao,' he
yelled to his runner and then, fixing Dar with a benevolent
smile, broke into a sher from a book he had been gifted by
his girlfriend and was currently trying to memorize. 'Wo

aaye ghar hamare, khuda ki zehmat hai; kabhi ham khud ko, kabhi apne ghar ko dekhte hain.'

The SHO coughed politely. 'The word is "kudrat", sir. Not "zehmat". Zehmat means annoyance.'

'I am so extremely sorry, SHO Sahab. I meant that only. Aap bataiye, kaise aana hua.' Bat Ball directed a look of concern at him.

Dar proceeded to open the carton he was carrying and laid out on Batabyal's table a dozen empty AK-47 cartridges. All of them were embossed with Pakistan Ordnance Factory logos. He then proceeded to give Batabyal a scene-by-scene account of the militant attack on his chowki the night before.

'I am shocked,' Bat Ball pronounced at the end of it. Ringing the bell for his runner, he summoned Dogra and Raizada to his office. 'And why hasn't the sevai come till now?' he snapped. 'Has the cook gone off to milk the cows? Chai bhi lao SHO Sahab ke liye. Aur mere liye bhi.'

The sevai, chai, Dogra and Raizada—all arrived in quick succession. While the SHO concentrated on savouring the dessert, Batabyal apprised the two new entrants with what had taken place barely five kilometres from their company post the night before. 'This is shameful,' he told Dogra. 'These militants are getting too big for their boots. How dare they attack a police post in our area? I will not tolerate this.' He sounded very upset. The SHO looked up, appeased.

Dogra had a deep frown on his forehead. 'Shocking indeed, sir,' he said. 'We must immediately conduct village searches. That is where these rats take shelter.'

'Raizada Sahab, you do so many village searches. Why are you not able to catch any militants?' Batabyal had now directed his annoyance at the towering Bhim Singh, much to the SHO's satisfaction.

'Sahab, Larnu police chowki does not send men with us. We had to call off our last two operations,' Raizada muttered darkly.

'You will not face that any more,' the SHO said, with remorse and guilt in his voice. He looked up at Raizada's handlebar moustache and scowling face and continued, 'These militants have crossed their limits. I assure you, Major Sahab, now onwards there will be complete cooperation from the local police. We will send men with your party at half-hour notice, whenever you ask.'

Batabyal looked serious. 'Jaiye aur apna kaam itminaan se kariye. I promise you, there shall be no more attacks on your police chowki,' he said.

All three stood by politely as the SHO got up to leave with a 'Khuda hafiz!' They watched him being escorted by the guard till right outside the company main gate, where his jeep was waiting. Batabyal turned around to find Raizada and Doggy looking at him with deadpan faces. 'Raizada Sahab, there should not be any more attacks on their chowki,' he declared, his voice stern.

'Theek hai, sa'ab. Nahi karenge,' Raizada replied, sending both Dogra and Batabyal into fits of raucous laughter.

'I think we have finally won his heart,' Batabyal declared, adding, 'Just make sure we alter our records to adjust the Pakistan Ordnance Factory ammunition captured from militants that was used up last night.'

'Already done, sir,' the efficient Doggy replied. With crisp salutes to their Company Commander, both he and Raizada turned around and, with wide smiles on their faces, walked out of the office.

The Secret

'Bhains ki aankh!' Major Somnath Batabyal, or Bat Ball, exclaimed loudly, making the sentry outside his office, who had only just dozed off to peaceful sleep, wake up with a start.

Steadying his shaking fingers to stop his mug of scalding hot langar chai from spilling over, the Bravo Company Commander of 13 Para placed it carefully on the table. Even in the Kashmir winter, he could feel fine beads of sweat popping up on his forehead. 'I can't believe this. Get him back to camp right now,' he said, ending the radio exchange with a furious 'Over and out!'

Dressed as most soldiers do while serving incognito in troubled Kashmir, Bat Ball sat in his muddy-brown phiran with his long, curly locks falling over his face, the dead wireless set still in his hands. His long-lashed eyes were fixed on the glowing bukhari that had warmed the room to a cosy twenty-six degrees. But the heat no longer appeared

to be reaching him, and he could feel his fingers slowly
turning cold.

* * *

Just a few hours back, his company had received an
intel that four armed militants were hiding in a deserted
dhok (animal shelter) just four kilometres away. Without
wasting time to get official clearance, he had immediately
dispatched a team of twelve paratroopers with strict
instructions to surround the hut and ask the militants to
surrender. 'If they start firing back, use a rocket launcher
to blow the dhok down. I don't want any casualties,' he
had instructed the Junior Commissioned Officer heading
the patrol, to which Subedar Bhim Singh Raizada, a big,
intimidating man, had responded with a characteristically
booming, 'Ho jaayega, sahab.'

After withdrawing weapons from the armoury and
putting on their helmets and bulletproof vests, the party
had left. It was getting dark, but they knew the area like
the back of their hands and were familiar with the exact
position of the suspected dhok—a solid log structure with
vegetation growing on its top—where the militants were
believed to have taken sanctuary. When they reached the
suspected location, Raizada informed Bat Ball that they
had laid out a cordon with three teams, of four men each,
covering the hut from three directions. He said that there
did not appear to be any signs of anybody being there.

Batabyal trusted Raizada Sahab's experience and asked him to check once and return to the unit. He then asked his sahayak to get him dinner from the mess, having decided to eat it on his office table. The wall clock in his office showed the time as past midnight. Batabyal had no plans to retreat to his room before his men returned safely.

Soon after he finished eating, grimacing over the thick rotis and the tasteless bottle-gourd curry on the menu, Batabyal asked his buddy to get him a big mug of sweet and strong ginger tea from the cookhouse. 'Chini thok ke, dudh rok ke,' he instructed clearly, adding a warning for the cook. 'Tell Bhanwari Lal to see me tomorrow. Bloody pathetic khaana he is making these days. He needs to go on a few long-range patrols,' Bat Ball growled.

The tea quickly appeared and he had just taken a sip when the radio set buzzed. Raizada Sahab was on the line. 'Thoda bad news hai, sahab, aur thoda good news,' he said, adding, 'Ram Chander ko goli lag gayi hai, aur Bacchi Singh bhi zakhmi hai. But the good news is that both are out of danger.'

Bat Ball took it on the chin. 'Koi baat nahi, sahab. Hota hai operations mein. How many militants were there inside the dhok?' he asked.

There was a long silence, after which Raizada sheepishly replied, 'Ek bhi nahi tha, sahab.'

'How did our men get shot then?' Batabyal asked incredulously.

'IFF mein thodi gadbad ho gayi, sahab,' Raizada replied, using the military abbreviation for 'Identification Friend or Foe'. 'It was pitch-dark. We saw four armed men in phirans moving stealthily behind the hut and opened fire suspecting them to be militants. It turned out they were our own team members who had changed location without informing me.' Raizada Sahab then charmingly added, 'Galti se mishtake ho gaya, sahab.'

Batabyal could see the room swirling before his eyes. He knew he was a doomed man. First, because he had sent a team out on an anti-militant operation without informing his Commanding Officer. And second, because his company had shot their own men. He could feel his ears turning red-hot at the very thought of breaking the news to Colonel Jang Bir Singh, Vir Chakra, his Commanding Officer, aka Krur Singh.

More than six feet tall with broad shoulders, large fiery eyes, a fierce moustache and a deep voice, Krur Singh spoke flawless English as well as exquisite Urdu, splattered with the most imaginative expletives that rolled off his tongue with careless abandon. Contrary to his appearance, however, he was a gentle, gregarious man in peacetime situations, known for taking youngsters out for dinner to the best restaurants, always insisting on picking up the tab himself. Or, inviting them home on the weekend, feeding them the best mutton lababdaar that he would himself cook in desi ghee, sliding in and out of the kitchen with a double scotch on the rocks in his hands, brushing aside accusations from the pretty and petite Mrs Singh about drinking too much with a gruff 'Arre! Kya baat kar rahi ho! This is only my second drink. You can ask the boys.' To which the boys had been trained to nod obediently.

Besides Mrs Singh, whom he had eloped with seventeen years back, his daughter, Gunnu, who was studying fashion design in Paris and his Maruti 800 that stood proudly beside his new Range Rover, the loves of his life were his three handsome double-coated German Shepherds that he walked every evening, taking them minus the leash and thus ensuring that Mall Road was free of pedestrian traffic from 5–6 p.m. Though he called them his gentle babies not capable of hurting even a fly, the entire cantonment was terrified of their intimidating appearance. And of his.

But the truth was that Col Jang Bir Singh was a perfect gentleman. It was only when he put on his uniform that he underwent a complete transformation and took on his Krur Singh avatar. With red tabs blazing on the collars, his maroon beret on his head and the CO's baton in his hands, he metamorphosed into the devil incarnate, with zero tolerance for any kind of shamming or incompetence. He was a brave, hardworking man and expected the same from his battalion. And now that the unit had moved to a non-family station in active Kashmir, his tolerance levels had dipped even further. The ground rules he had formulated for his men were, 'No one will lie. No one will try to act smart. Not a leaf shall stir in the regiment without my knowledge. And everyone—from CO to soldier—shall be sent home on leave every four months.' Bat Ball now feared that he might just be cashiered and sent home without pension.

* * *

Half an hour later, the crack team returned, bringing along the two casualties—Paratrooper Bacchi Singh, who had received a spray of pellets in his shoulder; and Paratrooper Ram Chander, who had a bullet injury in the thigh and was being carried on a makeshift stretcher fashioned from a groundsheet of waterproof tarpaulin stretched between two rifles.

Nursing Assistant Naik Dilbagh Singh, a sincere Sikh boy from Moga in Punjab, immediately put the moaning Ram Chander on a drip, injecting him with a strong painkiller and a tetanus shot. A concerned Batabyal, waiting outside the MI room, was relieved to hear that though the bullet had gone through Ram Chander's thigh, it had missed his bone, leaving a hole that Dilbagh Singh assured him would fill up on its own in a month or two. Bacchi Singh, he said, had a minor injury that would be fine in a few days.

* * *

Back in his office, Bat Ball could hear the birds chirping, declaring the onset of dawn, even though it was still dark.

He sat with his head in his hands, wondering how he was going to break the news to the CO. That was the state in which his Company Second in Command, the wise and wily Captain Amit Dogra, found him in when he rushed into Bat Ball's office in a phiran hastily thrown over his night suit, having learnt from the grapevine that the company had screwed up again, and this time royally so.

Bat Ball looked up at Dogra's cheerful 'Good evening, sir' and retorted with 'Morning ho gayi hai, Doggy', pointing at the wall clock that showed 4.30 a.m. 'Besides, there is nothing good about the morning. Kaand ho gaya hai company mein.'

Dogra shook his head in sympathy.

'Krur Singh will skin me alive,' Batabyal muttered despondently.

'Only if he hears of it, sir,' Doggy answered.

Bat Ball looked up to find Doggy's spectacles glinting and asked him incredulously, 'Are you trying to suggest that I should not tell him about the firing, Doggy?'

Dogra was biting his fingernails, which meant that his phenomenal brain was at work. 'I had a chat with the Nursing Assistant, sir. He said it is a superficial wound that will heal in two months. The CO need not see Ram Chander till then. What he doesn't know, he doesn't need to know.' Doggy was at his evil best.

Bat Ball looked at him in open-mouthed admiration.

Instructions were immediately passed down the rank and file that the shooting incident was being wiped off the daily event register and that no one was to breathe a word about it to anyone outside the company. The soldiers were happy to be part of Op Cover-Up, proud to be able to stand by their company in its hour of need.

That morning, the company briefing to the Commanding Officer lasted ten minutes, with Bat Ball not uttering a word about the botched-up covert operation. Later in the day, he ran into Ram Chander, who lay sprawled on the grass in the sparkling winter sunshine, loudly cheering the participants of a friendly volleyball match. There was a healthy pink glow on his face, and other than his bandaged leg (the trouser leg was cut off at the mid-thigh level), everything about him seemed relaxed and happy. Dilbagh had recommended a high-calcium and protein diet to him, and Ram Chander was being fed the juiciest chicken, the best eggs, bowls of curd and the largest glasses of warm condensed milk. No work duties had been assigned to him, and looking at him you could tell that his life had never been better.

* * *

The days started to pass very quickly. While the rest of Bravo Company sweated in the forests hunting for militants, Ram Chander was enjoying a paid holiday like never before. Finally, he was spanking new, with a small coin-sized scar as the only evidence of his injury. Bat Ball thumped Dilbagh on the back for a job well done and grinned at Ram Chander, telling him to go home on his leave, which was two months overdue.

The next morning, Ram Chander packed his bags and jumped on to a local bus. Two more jawans, also proceeding on leave, were with him. The three of them were dressed in phirans, blending with the local crowd. No army vehicles were used in the area, which was infamous as a site for IED blasts. Militants did not target local buses to avoid collateral damage, and that was why the army preferred to use these for travel here.

The bus rumbled its way past the twists and turns in the mud track, carrying the soldiers to their battalion headquarters, eighty kilometres away, where, unbeknownst to all the characters involved in the story so far, a dark twist in the tale awaited them.

* * *

Col Jang Bir Singh was a conscientious man, very particular about the standard unit drill called the 'CO interview' in army parlance, where both outgoing as well as incoming soldiers were invited to the CO's office for a brief one-to-one conversation. That afternoon, he looked up to find Paratrooper Ram Chander saluting him smartly. 'Kaisa hai, Ram Chander? Koi problem toh nahi?' the Colonel asked, looking down at Ram Chander's papers placed before him.

'Theek hai, sahab,' Ram Chander replied with a wide smile.

Col Jang Bir Singh was surprised to note that Ram Chander had last gone home six months back. 'Why didn't you take leave in four months?' he asked, smiling warmly. 'Biwi se jhagda toh nahi ho gaya?'

Delighted to find the CO joking with him, an overwhelmed Ram Chander replied, 'Goli lag gayi thi na, sahab, isliye nahi jaa paya.' The moment the words left his mouth, Ram Chander realized he had made a fatal mistake.

Krur Singh's large eyes had narrowed to fine slits. 'Goli! Kahan goli lagi, beta?' he purred, his voice soft and menacing.

A nervous, stuttering Ram Chander had no option left but to vomit out the complete truth.

The Colonel listened attentively, getting all the details clear in his head, and then dismissed him with the instruction that he should get his leg examined by the Regimental Medical Officer and only then proceed on leave. Ram Chander, relieved, saluted him and left.

* * *

Batabyal had just finished a heavy lunch of mutton curry and rice, followed by a big bowl of creamy sevai. After three days of punishment treks in the forest, the cook had regained his culinary expertise and was now dishing out the most sumptuous meals. Bat Ball was pleased. He was planning to lie down on the green slope in the sunshine and have an afternoon siesta when the radio set buzzed.

Major Navrang Apte, the Battalion Adjutant, was on the line. 'Oye hero!' he said. 'A soldier was shot in your company two months back and you did not inform the CO? Star hai tu saale!' He was chuckling wickedly. 'But sorry to say, the CO now knows and wants to speak to you.'

The radio set buzzed for a few seconds and Apte came back on the line with an evil 'You are now dead, Bat Ball'. Then, Batabyal heard the sound of deep, laboured breathing. 'Bravo Tiger for one five, over,' he squeaked.

'Friend!' Krur Singh's voice, seething with rage, sent a chill down Batabyal's spine even from eighty kilometres away. 'Report to my office tomorrow morning. Out.' Shaken and stirred, Bat Ball placed the receiver back on the instrument.

* * *

The next morning, at 4 a.m. sharp, Batabyal was sitting in a freshly acquired Tata Sumo, which had been crossing the company's main gate. He had put on a clean phiran, tried to comb some order into his long, curly hair and was accompanied by his QRT of two armed soldiers, also dressed like locals. The car's Kashmiri driver was enjoying some chai-nashta in the cookhouse, the day's wages deposited in his pocket, while his car keys had been taken over by Lance Naik Maqbool, the best driver in the company.

Bat Ball's heart was beating hard when he reported to the Adjutant's office. At 9 a.m. sharp, Col Jang Bir Singh arrived, and at 9.05 am, Batabyal was called in. No one knows exactly what transpired in the 'Tiger's Den' that morning, but Apte did not have to strain too hard to get a broad idea. The entire office could hear the burning expletives that re-established Krur Singh's credentials as someone with a legendary bilingual vocabulary. It is said that Bat Ball emerged thirty minutes later with his eyes blank, his ears bright red, wiping the sweat off his face with his big white-and-blue check handkerchief. The guard standing outside, accustomed to seeing the bravest of Company Commanders being reduced to quivering jelly by Krur Singh, saluted him and then discreetly looked away.

Fishing out his Aviator shades from his phiran pocket, Batabyal put them on as he marched down the corridor to locate Maqbool in the parking lot.

The Colonel Goes to Bangkok

Twenty minutes have passed since baggage collection at Suvarnabhumi Airport. So far, there is no sign of the Bangkok Taxi man who had promised online to take us Bangkoking over the next three days. Mom's and Aunt Uma's worry lines are deepening. Colonel Y.S. Rawat, 'Loin' to the family—an innocent mispronunciation of 'lion' and an ode to the legendary Hindi film villain Ajit ('sara sheher mujhe loin ke naam se jaanta hai')—has acquired the lips-tightly-stretched 'they're-all-bloody-cheats' look. Saransh, ten, is sulking because his PSP battery has died, and aspiring writer Isha, eleven, is looking sad and disheartened by the turn of events, which she had expected would inspire her debut bestselling novel. Cousin Tanu (Raa-bert to my Mike-ale in this trying assignment to take Loin and the family on a Southeast Asia tour) is rolling her eyes and mouthing 'Just chill' to me.

Just when I am done kicking myself for not having stuck a red rose behind an ear or at least painted a mole on my chin for easy recognition, I spot, in the swarming sea of faces, a placard at half mast, with a name on it that looks vaguely familiar: 'Mr Rachna Beast'. Is it my imagination or is the man half-heartedly holding up that placard really Adnan Sami (from before he had lost all that flab)?

Letting go of the trolley bearing a mountain of suitcases, I walk towards him and give him a wide smile, declaring, 'Hi! I'm Rachna.'

'You are Meestal Beast?' he asks incredulously.

'Well! Errr . . . Yes!' I nod firmly, telling myself that confidence is everything in cross-cultural confrontations. And I'm not wrong. His doubts are immediately dispelled.

'Welcome to Bangkok. I am Meestal Beeeeeg,' he booms and goes on to give me a handshake that feels like my hand has been swallowed by a wet, boneless jelly fish. I hastily withdraw my fingers and check to see if all of them are intact. Mom, who has been watching with an eagle eye, does not approve of this immodest fraternizing with an unknown man. I can sense an 'Apne Bharatiya Sanskar Mat Bhulo' talk coming up but ignore her for the time being. Meanwhile, Loin is trooping forth, arm outstretched. 'Mr Big, meet Colonel Rawat,' I introduce the two as Colonel Rawat's fingers close around Mr Big's, and the crunch and sudden squeak that escape the latter assure me that he now knows what manly handshakes are all about.

* * *

Now why would a decent Indian family go holidaying to a place famous for the kinds of things decent authors, like this one, shouldn't be writing stories about? Because it happens to be on the way to Bali, my dear reader. And Bali is where we are headed, with a flight change planned at Bangkok. Not only does it get us a cheaper flight, we also get some amazing rates on four-star hotels with buffet breakfast thrown in.

* * *

Mr Big drives us in a lovely luxury van to the hotel and then in the evening to the Siam Niramit show, which most people miss out on, no doubt distracted by the numerous other attractions of Thailand. Well, we don't. As the show unfolds, recounting Thai history and culture, rivers come gushing down the stage, large fishing trawlers make their way in, a thunderstorm erupts, apsaras drop from the skies and crops flower in front of our eyes. There's humour, romance, mythology thrown in, with some unbelievable acoustics and special effects.

The entire family watches spellbound, and for once the whiny kids are silent too, totally taken with the magnificent elephants that troop down the aisles, the grand court processions, the magic, the pretty *krathongs* that we are invited to set afloat in the water. It's an evening well-spent. The jetlagged ladies are smiling too. At the end of the day, Loin gives us—Raabert and me—a pat on our backs and roars, 'Damn good choice!' We click our heels and military salute.

* * *

The next morning the regiment is ordered to attack the buffet breakfast and gets down to the task with full *josh*. We stuff ourselves to bursting point with the buffet breakfast at the riverside restaurant and dig into some luscious local produce—passion fruit, snake fruit, pineapple, papaya and rambuthan (which turns out to be a sort of litchi with a more elaborate hairdo).

Then, we go looking for our luxury van at the hotel reception. Abracadabra! It has today turned into its poorer cousin. Mr Big has been replaced by someone who looks like Mr Small. We soon find that he is 'Meestal Meeth', who, as he reports to us, 'no speak Englees'. I am quite pleased that in my heels I can look down upon his five feet. But there has been a breach of contract, and I know that the Colonel shall have none of it.

Since Mr Mith cannot understand us, all communication will have to be done in sign language. Loin tries yelling in his ear, but that too does not seem to enhance his understanding of the English language. I am ordered to sort out the matter with Bangkok Taxi. Only then shall the regiment move ahead. While the others chill in the van, I call up Mr Suwan (CEO, Bangkok Taxi) and give him a piece of my mind.

'You no get angly my flaan,' he says, apologizing profusely before beginning a flattering monologue about India—the land of beauty and culture, of the loveliest women in the world, his best customers. He offers me special rates ('others I give less'), offers to change the taxi, change the driver, even offers to drive himself. He completely convinces me that he is shattered by our dissatisfaction with his services. My heart melts and I am ready to risk the Loin's wrath for him.

Just for the record, we continue with the same taxi service and driver throughout the trip, with the smooth-talking Mr Suwan distracting me completely each time I call to complain.

The kids get back to their PSPs, the ladies sleep off their breakfast and the Colonel resorts to third-degree methods to elicit information from Mr Mith. He plonks himself down on the passenger seat, much to Mr Mith's alarm, and starts talking to him in chaste Hindi, with a bit of Garhwali thrown in. When Raabert and I give him the 'what-are-you-doing-baas?' raised eyebrows, the Colonel says he has his own ways of catching lying cheats. If Mr Mith understands Hindi and/or Garhwali, he does a very good job of pretending he doesn't.

We are taken to the Damnoen Saduak floating market, the beautiful bridge on the River Kwai and the Tiger Temple at Kanchanaburi, where big, sleepy tigers are kept tied up in chains like pet dogs, and visitors can touch them and have their pictures taken. It upsets the animal lovers among us, and we decide to leave early.

* * *

On day three, we visit the awesome Temple of the Reclining Buddha, or Wat Pho, which dazzles us with its stunning architecture, brilliant colours and the Buddha's mother-of-pearl feet. Our charming guide, Suchin, tells us he is a cancer survivor and an ex-army man and insists on saluting the Colonel after each briefing, making the Loin's chest puff up a few more inches.

Then it's time to hit a mall—MBK Center or Mahboonkrong—where we look at some fake designer watches and pick up T-shirts and strappy sun dresses for a steal. Saransh is completely mesmerized by a keychain that is disgustingly designed to look like dog poo. The shopkeeper pretends to swallow it and burps loudly. Saransh, who is fascinated, digs his heels in and wails that he has to have the keychain. I pull him away callously.

Later in the evening, we take a dinner cruise on the Cho Phraya River, where we see the riverside sights of Bangkok, all beautifully lit up. The live band is playing some lovely Abba numbers. A buffet dinner awaits us. The Colonel switches on his legendary army charm and shakes a leg with the pretty Thai girls, completely outshining the paunchy Australian and Japanese tourists flashing dollar tips. Our regiment stands by and applauds him when he returns with a satisfied 'I have vanquished the enemy' look on his face.

On the drive back to the hotel, we cross an area where mats are laid out on the roadside and some kind of strangely nefarious activity is going on. I look around stealthily to see if anyone else has noticed the change of scenery to find that the kid, who I thought could only be surgically separated from his PSP, has his nose glued to the car window. 'What are they doing? What are they doing?' he whines.

Isha looks out of the window and starts taking copious notes, obviously meaning to add a chapter to her book. Mom is saying 'Hey Bhagwan' on a loop. Aunt Uma is sleeping, blissfully unaware that calamity has struck.

Mr Mith, noticing that interest has been generated, helpfully asks, 'You wan stop?' slowing down next to a fat man and a young girl engrossed in some complicated calisthenic moves.

Is it my imagination or has the Loin boxed the driver's ear? 'Abey! Aage badh . . .' he bellows, finishing the sentence with an unprintable, incestuous Hindi swear word. The shocked driver steps on the gas and the car zips ahead. 'Didn't I tell you he understands Hindi?' Loin says, looking back victoriously at me and Raabert.

Saransh is still whining: 'Wait! Stop! Mujhe dekhna tha.'

'Baby, that was Thai massage,' says Raabert, very smartly diverting the kid's attention.

Aunt Uma, who has only just woken up, says she wanted to have one too. Isha puts up her hand for another question, but Raabert distracts everyone by saying we need to go back and sleep since we have to get up a little after midnight for our early morning flight to Bali. 'We are going to go to the beach. We're going to snorkel. We're going to swim with the dolphins. We're going to have a great time in Bali,' she says.

Well, are we? If you are looking for answers to all those and other nail-biting questions—like, 'Does Saransh find something more interesting that his PSP in Bali?'; 'Does Isha get a plot for her novel?'; 'Does Mom find vegetarian food that doesn't smell of sea weed?'; 'Does the Colonel go for a body massage?'; 'Does the regiment vanquish Bali, too?'—watch out for the next book. But, of course, that shall happen only if the publishers get decent sales on this one.

Acknowledgements

I would like to thank my husband, Col Manoj Rawat, and our son, Saransh, for gifting me the peace of mind and contentment from which stories can sprout. My brother, Col Sameer Bisht, SM, VSM, for narrating those fascinating paratrooper tales that made me frown and smile and sometimes burst into laughter, and that led to many of the stories in this book. He also made south Kashmir and the Siachen Glacier come alive for me and helped me to flesh out (what I hope are) believable stories about places I have never seen, about people I have never met, except in my imagination.

I would also like to thank Prithvi Raj Banerjee—aka Earth Man, my classmate at St John's College, Agra, and a Massachusetts Institute of Technology scholar—for wading uncomplainingly through multiple versions of the same story with infinite patience and mailing me his feedback all the way from Boston.

I am also grateful to my book editor, Gurveen Chadha, for her unflinching support, for the brainstorming sessions when we tried to decide the tone the book would take and the stories it would include, and for dispelling my apprehensions about readers expecting only stories of heroism with a confident, 'Authors decide what stories they want to tell.'

Thanks to Penguin Random House India's creative head, Ahlawat Gunjan, for his complete involvement in designing this beautiful cover, which made me worry if my stories would deliver on the content it promises.

And last, but certainly not the least, I would like to thank Vineet Gill, whose brilliant editing and personal involvement with the stories made them way more crisp and riveting than what the first drafts looked like. Thank you, Vineet, for ruling like the proverbial iron hand in velvet glove.

Though it is only my name that you read on the cover, this book actually belongs to all of us.